USA TODAY BESTSELLING AUTHOR

Dale Mayer

TERKEL'S TEAM SERIES

DAMON'S DEAL

BOOK 01

DAMON'S DEAL: TERKEL'S TEAM, BOOK 1
Beverly Dale Mayer
Valley Publishing Ltd.

Copyright © 2021

ISBN-13: 978-1-773364-96-4
Print Edition

Books in This Series:

Damon's Deal, Book 1
Wade's War, Book 2
Gage's Goal, Book 3
Calum's Contact, Book 4

About This Book

Welcome to a brand-new series from *USA Today* best-selling author Dale Mayer, where dark-ops SEALs have special senses and skills, needed to solve intrigue, betrayal, and … murder. A series with all the elements you've come to love, plus so much more, … including psychics!

With the bulk of his team down, Terk tries to establish a new base, while struggling to heal the team through the special connection each has. Damon is concerned about finding Tasha, one of their admins, and keeping her safe. But, without any secure place to take her, Damon's making do with the little they have—whether she's happy about his plan or not.

Tasha, barely surviving an assassination attempt, is not sure who to trust. When Damon comes to check on her, she can only hope her instincts and her heart are right about him. This man meant everything to her for the years they'd worked together, but he'd always kept her at arm's reach. Now to learn that he and Terk are the only fully cognizant members of her old team, she wants to help but doesn't want to risk her life … again.

Still struggling with their new reality, both Tasha and Damon need to find out who did this to them. It's the only way to get their lives back—and to have a future together …

Sign up to be notified of all Dale's releases here!
https://geni.us/DaleNews

CHAPTER 1

ICE POURED HERSELF a coffee and sat down at the compound's massive dining room table with the cup. When her phone rang, she smiled at the number displayed. "Hey, Terk. How're you doing?" She put the call on Speakerphone.

"I'm okay," Terkel replied, his voice distracted and tight. "Barely."

"Terk?" Merk called from across the table. He got up and walked closer and sat across from Levi. "You don't sound too good, brother. What's up?"

"I'm fine." Terk paused. "Or I will be. Right now, things have blown to shit."

"As in literally?" Merk asked.

"The entire group, … they're all gone. I had a solid team—seven like me—and they're all gone."

"Dead?" Ice's jaw dropped in shock.

Several others stood to join them, gathered around Ice's phone. Levi stepped forward, his hand on Ice's shoulder. "Terk? Are they all dead?"

"No." Terk took a deep breath. "I'm not making sense. I'm sorry."

"Take it easy." Ice's voice remained calm and reassuring. "What do you mean, *they're all gone*?"

"All their abilities are gone," he stated. "Something's

happened to them. Somebody has deliberately removed whatever supersenses they could utilize—or what we have been utilizing for the last ten years for the government." His tone was bitter. "When the US gov recently closed us down, they promised that our black ops department would never rise again, but I didn't expect them to attack us personally."

"What are you talking about?" Merk asked in alarm, standing up now to stare at Ice's phone. "Are you in danger?"

"Maybe? I don't know," Terk replied. "I need to find out exactly what the hell's going on."

"What can we do to help?" Ice asked.

Terk gave a broken laugh. "That's not why I'm calling. Well, it is, but it isn't."

Ice looked at Merk, who frowned as he shook his head. Ice knew he and the others had heard Terk's stressed-out tone and the completely confusing bits and pieces coming from his mouth. Ice spoke next. "Terk, you're not making sense again. Take a breath and explain. Please. You're scaring me."

Terk took a long slow deep breath. "Tell Stone to open the gate," he said. "She's out there."

"Who's out there?" Levi asked, looked outside, and shrugged.

"She's coming up the road now. You have to let her in."

"Who? Why?" Ice asked.

"*Because* ... she's harnessed with C-4."

"Jesus." Levi bolted to display the camera feeds on the big screen in the dining room. "Is it live?"

"It is, and she's been sent to you."

"Well, that's an interesting move," Ice noted, her voice sharp, activating her comm to connect to Stone in the control room. "Who's after us?"

"I think it's rebels within the Iranian government. But it could be our own government. I don't know anymore," Terk snapped. "I also don't know how they got her so close to you. Or how they pinned your connection to me," he added. "I've been very careful."

"We can look after ourselves," Ice replied immediately. "But who is this woman to you?"

"She's pregnant," he explained, "so that adds to the intensity here."

"Understood. So who is the father? Is he connected somehow?"

There was silence on the other end.

Merk said, "Terk, talk to us."

"She's carrying my baby," Terk replied, his voice heavy.

Merk, his expression grim, looked at Ice, her face mirroring his shock. Merk asked, "How do you know her, Terk?"

"Brother, you don't understand," Terk stated. "I've never met this woman before in my life." And, with that, the phone went dead.

CHAPTER 2

D AMON WILCOX STARED as Terkel slowly lowered his phone, his attention still on the screen in front of him. That was a hard conversation. Damon could only imagine the reaction on the other end of that phone right now. "What do you think they'll do?"

"I think"—Terkel raised his gaze to look at Damon— "No, *I know* that they'll let her in."

"It's a risk for all of them," he reminded his old friend.

Terkel nodded. "Yes, it is, but I have faith in who they are as people. That woman didn't deserve what those assholes did to her."

"We don't even have a name, do we?"

"Celia," he noted quietly. "That's all I know."

Damon nodded slowly. "And while they are looking after her"—he watched as Terk started texting on his phone again—"where do you want us to start?"

Terk looked at him, the briefest of smiles on his face. "You need to focus on regaining your abilities. Of everybody, you're the one who appears to have most of them. Or at least didn't lose them all."

"No." Damon frowned at that and stared off in the distance. "I can feel something." He paused. "I don't know what it is—maybe a block, maybe a burn or a scar through my sight or something. I don't know. But I can sense something foreign."

"Foreign? As in something inside you?" Terk asked sharply.

Damon sighed. "I can't explain it." He looked at his friend curiously. "And you don't have any disruption in your talents?"

"No, but I was off-line, doing some … maintenance," he noted, for lack of a better word. "That's when I noticed you guys were all slowly going down."

"Yet we weren't even all in the same place when this happened," Damon reminded Terk. "We were spread out all over town, like always when we're busy."

"I know," Terk agreed. "That's why I've always kept you guys on my radar, on a mental map of sorts."

Damon nodded. "I get it. I know all about that system. We've used a similar one to keep track of people, while they are out on jobs."

"Exactly, and it's a mental system, so, therefore, when I sense something happening," he explained, "I shut down my own senses."

At that, Damon's gaze widened.

Terk nodded. "I know. Don't think I didn't feel like I was betraying you. Believe me when I say, it wasn't an easy decision, but I knew I had no choice."

Damon immediately shook his head. "Hell no," he argued. "Self-preservation is always at the top of all our priority lists. What I was reacting to was the fact that you could sense it happening. That was huge."

"Only if I could have sensed it enough ahead of time to do something useful. And I really think it was due to the disconnection that I noticed."

Damon got up and paced the small room, empty except

for the table and the electronics. It was a warehouse storage compound. In their warehouse, they had one fully concrete room to themselves. Nobody else in this area knew who they were or what they were doing. But the concrete had been important for their own abilities, a place where they might actually relax. It should be steel, six inches of thick steel *and* concrete. But they didn't have that resource available to them anymore.

They used to be part of a special black ops team, working for the US government. The program was being disbanded, and, on the last day, a lovely coincidence was that everyone, not Terk, but the seven other men on the team started to experience agonizing pain and a complete wipe of their senses. Or at least Damon assumed it was complete. From what Terk had said, it sounded like it was, as Damon knew two of the men were in comas, two of the men were coming back out of a similar state, and two were … presumed lost on the ethers. Terk, as the boss himself, was in the best shape of all. Wade was, in a way, fighting hard to heal and to regain some consciousness, like Damon had been not too long ago. "I'm not sure why I didn't get hit as hard as the others," Damon murmured. "My instinctive thought was because I wasn't as much of a danger."

Terk snorted. "You guys are all dangerous to anybody who knows what we can do."

"And yet we aren't terribly powerful."

"We're more powerful as a team," Terk acknowledged quietly. "But still individually, you each have specific talents."

"But individually, we all have the ability to connect or see or feel or sense various things at a very long distance. And most of our work has been done on government jobs."

Damon shook his head. "I still can't believe our government disbanded our group."

Terk stiffened, turned, looked at his friend. "I have to suspect that, due to the timing, they're the ones behind this."

Damon slowly nodded. "I wondered if you would come to the same conclusion as I did."

"Absolutely," Terk snapped. "But it's only guesswork at the moment. A gut feeling. We need to investigate. Plus, the department wouldn't have done this themselves. They'd have contracted the job out. But who and how?"

"Whatever they did, it's continuing to affect the team." Damon studied his friend, then decided to ask the question in the back of his mind. "So you have an ability to filter into each and every one of the team's psyches?"

"Sometimes to transmit messages, sometimes just to check up on their health," Terk admitted. "I can do a bit more, but it's limited."

"I've always known that to some degree," Damon admitted. "We've discussed it slightly but never in detail."

"And that was partly on purpose," Terk stated, "because it seemed like I was pushing the line by getting into their heads at all."

"I don't know about that. I don't think anybody hated you for it, and I did speak with a couple of them because they could sense when you put in the messages that you were also taking a look around. And your telepathic abilities have always been phenomenal."

"That was a two-second mental check, like, 'Hey, on a scale of one to ten, how is this guy doing?' And then getting a response and getting out." Terk smiled.

"Even in mine?" Damon asked, a sharp look at his friend.

"Even yours," Terk agreed with a nod. "We are part of a team, and keeping the team safe, healthy, and functioning is always my goal."

"And, because we understood that, it was fine," he agreed. "Can you communicate with any of them now?"

"Wade, yes, but he is not capable of responding, yet I sense brain activity. As for the others, I know they're there, but I'm not getting even that."

"Are you getting *any* response?"

"Like a life-support system," Terk noted. "Other than that, not a whole lot."

"Well, that's a start. We have to make sure that we keep them safe." Damon frowned. "But that kind of security may need to be physical," Damon said. "Keeping them safe on the energy level is a different matter, not to mention we don't know what happened in the first place. We have to stop a second attack."

"And that's what I've been trying to do," Terk confirmed quietly. "I know it's like closing the barn door after the fox got in," he admitted, "but I've got a psychic guard around each of the team members. Less around you because you are recovering."

"And Wade?"

"On a scale of one to ten, I'd say his health is at a five, so 50 percent. If I can even get that inched up to 52 to 53 percent, he's heading in the right direction. The problem is, I can't maintain this level of energy around everybody alone."

"And I can't help you and be on the hunt," Damon replied.

"I know, so somehow we have to sort our priorities."

"No." Damon shook his head. "Somehow we have to get

help."

At that, Terk raised an eyebrow. "I don't know who you're expecting to come help us. We don't have any government-sanctioned assistance anymore, and very few can help at this level."

"I know, and that just sucks too because we need resources."

"Money is not an issue," he reminded him. "We have plenty of that."

"And that's a damn good thing," Damon noted, "because we need it all. Particularly with this kind of a security issue."

"No, I hear you," he agreed. "I'm just not exactly sure where to turn."

Damon hesitated for a moment. "What about your brother?"

Terk looked at Damon sharply, then frowned. "If I asked, he would come," but his reluctance was very telling.

"You don't want to put him in danger, do you?"

"Of course not," he admitted. "My brother and I have always been close, but, more than that, not many people out there understand or even accept me for who and what I am, like my brother does."

"But you're twins too, right?"

"We are." He nodded. "With one very important difference."

"He has no abilities?"

"None. We didn't even realize I did, until I hit about nine or ten."

"*Huh.* What if he has abilities now?" Damon asked. "And, if he does, and they're latent, that's an entirely different issue."

"Very latent. He's never been tested and has never shown any interest in being tested."

"Yet, as long as he's been supportive of you, maybe we can utilize that."

"And again, it would not be my choice. Anybody who even has any inkling of what we're doing still doesn't understand the kind of predators that we're dealing with. How could anyone? Although my brother would more than most."

"Do you think somebody else can do what we do?" Damon asked instantly.

"We took care of that—right? In Iran? But, if there was one group, maybe there are others."

"I'm not sure." Damon slowly reached up to rub his temples.

"And because my energy is split, trying to individually funnel a guard around our team, I don't have the power I need to defend you and me properly."

"And that is not acceptable," Damon snapped. "I get we have to save everybody, but you are the strongest of us all. We must have you at the forefront of every investigation in order to make it all work."

"Well, that's the theory," Terk agreed, "but each and every one of us will have to pull a little bit more, if we can."

"You know we might need to bring in Wade, regardless of whether he's fully healed or not."

"And that could kill him," Terk replied instantly.

"It might." Damon hesitated. "Look. I know. I don't want to do it either, but, if he can do anything, even if just run basic comms for us, so that we can get out and start hunting, then he needs to." He could see that Terk was torn. "Maybe think about it from his perspective. Right now you're saying he's completely useless, even though so many other people out there would say that, even without his extra abilities, he is a hell of a better man than most."

"He absolutely is," Terk noted quietly. "But I also know that the more he drains his energy, the less he'll utilize to help us, and, with his energy drained, it will stop his healing. Not to mention he's slowly waking, but he's not conscious. And yanking him out of that state could kill him."

"Dammit," Damon muttered because Terk was correct. But when did this stop and start being something that they could utilize in a different way? "We have to do something," he replied. "We're sitting ducks right now."

"We've already been taken down," he stated. "What we have to do is keep anybody from finding out that we may not recover from this." And then he stopped and whispered, "Not all of us, but maybe a few of us."

"Do you really think not everybody will recover?"

"I don't want to say," he murmured. "But, in some cases, we're definitely on low life support."

Frowning, Damon stared at the table and the tablet of notes. "Where do we start?"

"I'd say Iran, in the cell that we shut down, doing the same kind of work as we are doing, but of course for the other side."

"And how many other sides are there now?" Damon snapped bitterly. "It seems like we're up against the Russians and the Chinese all the time. Now you're saying Iran."

"And I can't say for sure it's them. It could all be connected." He took a slow deep breath. "And it could be connected to our bosses."

Damon leaned back, dropped the pencil. "I know, and that means that we need to investigate them and Iran, while keeping an eye on China and Russia. And we don't have anybody to help us do that."

"I can bring in some help," Terk replied. "I don't think our three admins are doing anything right now. We all went our separate ways that night, with the expectation of the team getting in touch in a few days. Only we never got that chance." He cast Damon a raised eyebrow.

Damon realized who he was talking about. "Interesting." He hated the idea. He didn't want her in any more danger than she already was. "I'm not so sure that that's even a wise idea."

"But at least they understood what we were doing, and we still need people to run searches and people to do tracking."

Damon frowned, still not liking the idea. "You mean Tasha. She was good at that."

"I'll contact her. I think they're still working for the government though, and, if we don't want the government to know that we're alive and well …" Terk raised his eyebrows.

Damon shook his head. "Tasha was given her walking papers the same day the government shut us down."

"Why?" Terk asked in surprise.

"Mostly I think because of the connection to us."

"Has anybody talked to her since? I haven't." Terk looked at Damon.

"Neither have I." Damon immediately snatched up his phone. "If they killed off our abilities, hoping that they would completely close down the department," he noted with emphasis, "what are the chances that they did something to permanently injure her?"

"Well, they sure as hell better not have. We had three great hackers, IT staff. Let's see if we can find any of them."

"I'll check in with Tasha."

Terk nodded. "I'll contact Wilson, and then we'll have to look for Mera."

"Yes, and, if any or all three of them want to come back and work for us while we sort this out, we need them. That just brings back one other issue." Damon turned toward Terk. "When we got shut down, they removed our access, I presume?"

"Yes, access to databases, access to security, access to everything."

"What about the bank accounts?"

Terk gave him a ghost of a smile. "Yeah, that's not happening."

"Will they accuse you of stealing?"

"I highly doubt it because they didn't know about it in the first place." He was torn on that because, of course, that was in theory how it was supposed to be. "It was access we had before anyway."

"What are the odds that this annihilation was actually done because of that money? How much money are we talking about?" When Terk gave him a ballpark figure, Damon whistled silently. "We could have all been targeted just to get access to the money. Hell, they hide our budget from Congress so nobody without the highest of clearances knows what we're up to. This money is dark. Someone steals it, and who'd be the wiser? If it would never openly go into the government coffers because they didn't know about it, because it was hidden money, maybe someone *did* know and decided to get it for themselves."

"It's possible, but they could have done that without taking us out," he reminded Damon. "We would never have known once we were ousted."

"No, that's quite true. But still, it makes me suspicious."

"Anytime big money's involved, it makes us all suspicious," he murmured.

"Yeah, that is very true." His fingers were already redialing Tasha's number. But, so far, no answer. He bolted to his feet. "I don't like anything about this. I'll run over to her place."

"If she's still there. Remember. The bosses knew that we had some abilities, but they didn't really know all of what we did."

"No, they knew exactly what we did. They just didn't always understand the nuances of how we did it."

"Okay, good enough," Terk agreed. "I don't have a problem with that definition. Use your connection with Tasha to bring her back."

Damn it. How did he know? Terk was like that. He knew things—that no one should know. Damon pocketed his phone and shook his head at that. "I just want to make sure that I find her alive."

Terk's smile fell away. "Yeah, I hear you there." Just then he got a text, and he frowned. "I need to handle this."

As Damon went to walk out the door, he turned back to Terk. "Anything I need to know?"

"Not necessarily. My brother is about to call."

"Ah, well, let me know, and don't forget we could use the additional manpower."

Terk eyed him knowingly and then slowly nodded. "It is what they do. So maybe. I'll talk to my brother and see."

"Remember. They're already involved. *She's* there."

"You go look for Tasha. I'll talk to my brother."

With that, Damon exited. Outside, he hopped into a black truck—nondescript, beaten up, slightly dirty, with nothing to cause any attention. He drove out of the huge compound of warehouses and headed to the address he had on file for Tasha. He didn't bother calling again. Besides, this would need to be personal.

It didn't mean it was still the current address though, and that was a bit of a concern. They'd never gotten personal on the job, and he had deliberately kept it much less than personal. Mostly because of the heavy attraction. Personal relations on the job never worked out. However, they weren't on the job anymore, and that was even more dangerous because whatever the hell had happened had affected their whole team.

Only two days ago this had all come down; Damon had barely even surfaced when he found out that Terk was alive, and so they immediately banded up to try to find the rest of their team. What they'd found had been horrific.

The phone call to Levi's team, warning them about Celia's arrival, had been heartbreaking when all of them had realized what was going on. And even that knowledge came from Terk's psyche. And, of course, the text message saying that she was carrying something special had Terk sending out a probe and finding out the truth; she was carrying his child.

When he realized it was his own child, they had just sat here in stunned fury, realizing just how much somebody was playing games of life and death with the next generation. And one of the reasons why Terk's team had been disbanded was all over the arguments inside the government of how dangerous the group was. It should have been an easy job to shut down their operation, but now it looked way too much like the government had plans to shut them all down in another way too.

Yet why Celia? Surely that didn't play into the government's shut-down orders?

Damon understood, he really did, because to anybody in black ops oversight, who knew what Terk's team could and would do was terrifying. But, if they thought they would shut down and injure this entire team, like they had in an attempt to cover the behinds of some bureaucrats, they had another think coming. That would never be something this team agreed to.

Terk was the most powerful of them all, and yet, at the same time, he was also the most exposed because he had family. It was one thing to have a team like they did, but, with families to intimidate or to use as blackmail threats, it became a whole different ball game.

Especially now with this woman and Terk's unborn child.

Damon had no family. He had been abandoned at birth and had no clue who anybody was. He was raised in foster homes until he was old enough to join the military, all the while realizing something very strange was going on, so he cultivated it. Only when Terk had showed up at his door about eight years ago and had suggested that Damon come to work for him did he realize anybody else like him was out there. Since then, the two of them had been like brothers.

That it was possible that not all of them would regain their senses or potentially even survive was just devastating. Every one of them had a different ability, and some that they shared. Most of them could see either a location or people somewhere else, could communicate from another location, often on the other side of the world. Some of them could do so much more. And the longer they worked together, the more their individual skills improved.

That was one thing Damon could do. As long as he had something from that person, just a picture even, he could connect to wherever they were, sometimes talk to them, although they weren't necessarily amiable to psychic communication. Most of them thought he was speaking inside their head and thought they were going crazy. He'd learned a few tricks to help them believe, but it made his job that much more challenging. But, if he could get them to provide information to help a rescue go down, it was all worthwhile.

However, once the government found out more of what they could do, there had been a big push to annihilate the program. And maybe the team itself, in order to have their gifts no longer available to be exploited. And, of course, that was just the brass speaking.

Damon had always wondered whether his job would end in a good way or he would get out of this industry in a box. He finally figured out that it would be in a box, and whether he liked it or not didn't really matter because, when you knew the stuff that he knew, nobody out there would let him live.

Particularly when it came to the government.

He had absolutely no doubt in his mind that his own government was behind the attack on them. But proving it and getting payback or at least stopping somebody else from trying a repeat attack was a whole different story. The biggest problem would be finding out how this was done. And how could he protect himself and his team from a future attack?

He had an ability to help others and had utilized it to rescue many people. To think that somebody out there could shut them down on an energy level and could put them in a coma at a whim was scary. Whoever was capable of doing this had to be stopped, and unfortunately, in this case,

Damon could only see that those people would have to be permanently stopped. There couldn't be any other way because that threat would always stay out there on the horizon, and there would be no peace for Terk's team ever. Not exactly something Damon was willing to let happen.

And, on that note, he headed down the street in his nondescript black truck, punched in Tasha's address to his GPS, and followed it to his destination. There he stopped and stared up at the high-end apartment building, with full security features.

"Why an apartment?" he murmured. Except, given the work she did, maybe it was for safety. And then again, given the work she did, maybe she'd become a pain to the dark side. Was she even here? Or had she run to the Caribbean? He might not have answers now, but he would sure as hell find out.

TASHA MILLWORK PEERED through the curtains, watching the road outside of her apartment building. She watched as Damon slipped from the truck, his gaze ever wary, as he casually walked down the block, crossed, and then slipped into the back entranceway of her building. She raced to the apartment door with an ear against it, then listened quietly as she mentally thought about him coming up the stairs and crossing the hallway. No doubt he was coming to her, but the question was, *Why?* She'd never had reason to distrust him; then she'd never had reason to distrust anything until two days ago.

Two days ago she realized she was being followed. The same night somebody broke into her apartment, and she thought she heard footsteps cross toward her bedroom and had just enough time to push aside the covers and disappear onto her balcony, right when the bullets fired into her bedding. And, with that, the footsteps had raced away. She hadn't slept since. She also hadn't changed the door lock. Which meant that they could come back at any time.

But all of her contact numbers in the government no longer reached anybody. No answer at the end of anything. She didn't know what the hell had happened to her team either. She had known that they were due to be disbanded on that day and that was essentially the last day of work, but she had hoped to stay in touch with them, especially Damon. But given the circumstances, she knew it would take a few days; she'd been waiting eagerly, until bullets split her mattress.

Eagerness mixed with fear. Was he here to kill her? Or was he here to help her? She listened as the footstep strolled down the hallway—confident, sure, and powerful. When they stopped and knocked on the door across the hallway, she smiled.

When his low voice called out, "Tash, are you there?" her heart skipped a beat.

She looked down at her sweaty palms and wondered. Answering him could be the last thing she ever did. When she heard something at the other door, she peeked through the peephole to see him testing the knob, and, when it opened under his hand, he frowned, quickly glanced either way, and slipped into her apartment.

She swore. "I really should have fixed that damn door lock."

When he bolted out a little bit later, he was on his phone, and his face was stark white.

She heard him call somebody.

"Her apartment has been ransacked," he reported in a low voice. "Bullet holes are in her bed, but I found no sign of her and no blood. Kidnapped maybe?"

At that, she opened the door to the apartment across the hallway and poked her head out.

His gaze landed on hers, and he sucked in his breath. "No, I'll call you back. She's okay." He quickly slipped into the opposite apartment, shut the door, and stared at her.

She watched the emotions he wore on his face, as he reached out, grabbed her, and pulled her into his arms. When he held her close, she finally relaxed and burrowed in deeper. Thank God he was here for her.

"Dear God, when I saw the bullet holes …"

She reached up, gently stroked his cheek, and, when she could, she stepped back and swallowed hard. "What the hell is going on? Nobody is answering any phones. Nothing works anymore."

"I know. The entire team was attacked."

She stared at him in shock and wavered on her feet. He instantly picked her up, carried her to the couch, and plunked her down on the first cushion. "Deep breaths."

She tried hard; she really did, but it was almost impossible to breathe at all. "Are they … are they dead?" she finally got out.

He shook his head. "No, most are unconscious or struggling severely, two are in a deep coma," he murmured, "and we have no way of knowing whether they'll survive or not."

"Jesus." She closed her eyes and thought about the men she had worked with. "Do we know what happened?"

"No. … Terk is fine."

She laughed at that. "Of course he is," she said affectionately. "That man is invincible."

"Not quite," he argued. "I have to bring you up to speed on a lot."

She slowly nodded. "I get it, but I also need to tell you what happened here."

"Let's start with you."

She reiterated going to bed early but feeling off, and, when she heard somebody breaking into the apartment, she quickly pulled the pillows into the middle of the bed and, with the lights out, slipped onto the balcony. There, through the gaps in the curtains, she watched as the bedding bounced when the shots were fired into it. "I also heard some things getting tossed and turned, and then he was gone."

"Probably just making it look like a burglary gone bad." Damon reached out once again, grabbing her hands.

"Maybe, I don't know what the hell is going on though. I mean, we were supposed to be disbanded."

"What about you? Is that what you were supposed to do?"

"I thought I was moving back stateside," she explained. "I took an extra week here to maybe have a holiday, and then I would go see what my options were. They mentioned something about Homeland Security, if I wanted it. But honestly I think it was just talk." And how did she explain to him that she'd stayed around in case he contacted her? She just hadn't expected it to be like this. He frowned, but she shrugged. "I don't know why I would even go to a different department."

"And I'm not sure that was ever part of the plan," he stated. "Have you checked your emails?"

She nodded. "I can check my emails, but any email I send out to the government comes back as Undeliverable."

"And your phone?"

"Calls aren't going through at all."

He pulled a burner phone from his pocket and handed it to her. "Try with this phone. It's mine."

She looked at him in surprise.

"I don't know if you have been alienated because you work with us or if it's just your phone."

She frowned and quickly dialed one of the numbers that she knew by heart. When it went through, and a voice answered, she quickly hung up. She stared at him. "What does that mean?"

"It means that I think you've been alienated—or worse," he replied quietly, "just like the rest of us."

She stared at him, her jaw slowly dropping. "What?"

"The question is, where are the other two admins?"

"Oh my God." She shook her head. "I haven't talked to Mera or Wilson. I tried to call both of them, but I couldn't get through." With her burner phone, she quickly phoned Mera. When the other woman answered, her voice cautious, Tasha said, "Mera, this is Tasha."

"Oh my God, oh my God," Mera cried out, "where are you?"

"I'm still"—and then she stopped because Damon was shaking his head at her—"I'm safe, put it that way. But my apartment was attacked a few days ago."

"You too? Did they come in and shoot up your bed?" she asked bitterly. "I didn't move fast enough."

"Oh my God, are you hurt?"

"You could say that. Two bullets and I couldn't get anybody to answer to get help."

"Where are you?"

"At a friend's. I just …" And she stopped and started to

cry. "What's happening?" she asked. "Why did we get targeted?"

"I mean, the worst-case scenario," Tasha guessed, "is that somebody we were working against found us."

"I know. I know. I was thinking of that. But why is none of the team answering? I feel like we've been completely cut out."

"Have you talked to Terk at all?"

"No, but he was just at my door. But I'm not there. I went into hiding."

"How do you know?"

"Because I have an alarm set when my front door opens. And I saw his face go in and come out again, and he was pretty panicky."

Just then, as she said that, Damon's phone went off with a call from Terk. Damon got up and answered it. "Yes, she's here, and apparently Mera was also attacked. She's been shot twice but both minor. She's staying with a friend. She saw a video of you going into her apartment, but she didn't reach out because, like Tasha, she didn't know who the hell was after her. Now I'll find out where she is, and we'll collect her too." He put away his phone, turned, and look back at Tasha.

"I don't think she wants to be collected," Tasha noted quietly. "Mera, do you want to be collected?"

"I want to know what's going on." Her voice trembled. "And, although neither of my injuries are severe, I don't really want to be on the run right now. I don't know how we'll be protected because we've been cut off from all black ops support."

"Well, that's because none of us work there anymore," Tasha said bitterly. "Whoever targeted this attack chose a perfect day. Our last day."

"They did at that."

Tasha hesitated as Damon held out his hand. "Look. I've got Damon here. He'd like to speak to you."

"Damon? I thought they were all attacked."

Damon took the phone from Tasha's hand. "Mera, I'm sorry. We have all been attacked. Two of our team are in deep comas. Several others are in a half-and-half state. Terk and I, well, Terk is fine. I'm okay, but I've lost most of my extrasensory skills."

At that, Tasha sucked in her breath and reached out a hand.

"So I can tell you the attack was all encompassing. We're still trying to track down Wilson. Have you spoken to him?"

Mera was weeping on the other end. "I tried to call him, but I'm not getting any answer."

"Did you contact anybody in the government?"

"I contacted everybody," she cried out. "And it's like complete silence."

"That's exactly what it is," he agreed. "It is complete silence on all fronts. We are alone now."

"Oh my God, what did we *do*?"

"We didn't do anything, and what we have to figure out is who's behind it all."

"It's terrifying," she whispered. "I mean, I didn't expect to be attacked."

"None of us did." Damon's tone was a little harsh.

Tasha reached out a hand and frowned at him.

He closed his eyes, pinched the bridge of his nose, and nodded. "I'm just like everybody else. Terrified of what's going on. Scared to find out about the rest of the team."

"I'm staying where I am," Mera stated firmly. "You can

reach me at this number, but I need to heal."

"Tell me how bad it is." His order allowed no argument.

Yet Tasha heard the hesitation in her friend's voice.

"One in the shoulder and one in the thigh. Neither hit bone, only flesh, but I'm not up for running or in any fighting form."

"How will I know if you're safe?" he asked. "When I don't know where you are and I can't see you?"

"I know that is worrisome, but, right now, I know that I am safe, and that's got to be enough."

He hesitated. "I gather you don't trust me."

"I don't know whom to trust," she replied quietly, "so, for the moment, I'll just leave it as is."

"Fine, but please don't do anything, don't move, don't contact any more government bodies. Give us a chance to sort this out, and we'll get back to you."

"As long as you do," she stated, "because, believe me, it feels very much like everybody has forgotten we existed."

"I know. We're on it."

"Good luck," she replied quietly. "And take care of Tasha."

"I will, but we also have to find Wilson. If you hear from him, call me." And, with that, he gave her the new number on his phone and then handed the phone back to Tasha.

"Mera, take care of yourself, please. I'll go with Damon and see what we can sort out. They'll need somebody to run equipment."

"What equipment?" Mera asked. "Everything was shut down. Remember?"

"I know, and the office was cleared out overnight, according to Damon."

"Overnight? Well, that figures. We're black ops. Still,

you don't expect to be betrayed like this."

"No, and you can bet we'll find out what happened," Tasha stated. "Please look after yourself though."

And, with that, Mera hung up.

CHAPTER 3

DAMON LOOKED OVER at Tasha. "What are you doing over here?" he asked, his hand motioning to the area around them. "Do you own this apartment too?"

She winced. "I didn't know where else to go, and I was afraid the shooter would come back," she murmured.

Damon nodded encouragingly.

"So I did something I never thought I would do. I knew this couple were away on a holiday, so I picked the lock and came in."

"Picked the lock?"

"We do learn a few things in standard basic training."

He nodded. "Absolutely. I just hadn't realized you had learned anything important."

"Believe me. I haven't done very much with it at all. But I can certainly see the value now."

He winced. "I'm sorry about that."

"You really think we've all been terminated?"

It was hard to process, yet it fit. Even with what had happened to her. "Yes. The question is whether it was supposed to be all of us or if some of us were expected to survive."

"I'm thinking that everybody was supposed to be terminated. It's the only explanation for what happened to Mera and me."

"I think so too." He gave an absent nod, his expression far away.

"What are you thinking?"

"I'm worried about Wilson," he admitted. "He was new to the team."

"Worried or suspicious?"

He slid her a sideways glance. "Just for clarity, I'll always be suspicious of everything right now," he murmured, "until we get to the bottom of this."

She hesitated and then nodded. "He was new, but I think he was good. He was very good at what he did at least."

"Yes, and that can be used by other people. Everybody wants to capitalize on skills. And, like you and Mera, he had insider knowledge."

"I don't think he would have done anything deliberately to hurt us all."

"I hope you're right," he murmured, as he stood. "You coming?"

"Coming where?" she asked, looking at him. "Are you two organized? Have you a place for me? To live? To work? A secure place …"

He gave her a wolfish grin. "Well, let's just say that we'll be fine."

"If you say so," she murmured. She stood, looked around. "I really should make sure that nobody knows I've been here."

"Yep, we should, but chances are it's too late for that."

She frowned. "What do you mean?"

"Well, if you've been living here for a couple days …"

"Not quite."

"Right, then chances are you have already touched more

things than just the two of us can clear."

She frowned. "We don't have a clean-up team anymore, right?"

"No," he murmured, "not yet. We will have one set up again soon though."

"Let me get my things."

"Are they here?"

"Yes, I took everything that was important out of there and brought it here, in case I needed to run."

"Smart thinking," When she came out of the bedroom with one suitcase and a bag of personal stuff, he nodded. "It's still a bit much but not bad."

She snorted. "I wasn't exactly expecting to run on the fly. This was my home."

"And I'm sorry about that."

At least he sounded sincere. But the two to them had been studiously avoiding being too friendly for so long that it was a habit. What she really wanted was for him to hold her and to tell her it would be okay. Instead she said, "Well, I wasn't planning on staying anyway. That's what's so darn frustrating. You know? If we'd been told that we had to go home, it would be a different story."

"What it did, in this case, was to have you sitting in your place, nice and quiet, holing up for them to reach you."

"You mean, making me an easy target on purpose?"

He nodded slowly.

"Assholes," she muttered, as she took her suitcase to the front door. She looked around and swore. "I hope these people don't find out I was here."

"Hopefully they won't even notice. But, just in case, do you have a towel or something?"

She nodded, pulling one out, and they removed as much

of her fingerprints and tracks as they could. As she stood at the doorway afterward, she nodded. "It looks pretty good."

"What about your place?"

"Nothing to do. I threw out the bedding and flipped the mattress and ran. I didn't even look for bullets"

"They won't make much difference in this case he said quietly. "This was a pro job."

"The lease is up in a couple days, and it was a furnished apartment."

"Good enough, as long as you didn't leave anything behind."

She hesitated and then shrugged. "Maybe I better take another look." And, with that, they skipped across the hall into her apartment, where they did a quick walk-through.

"A few things are here," he noted.

She nodded, grabbed a garbage bag. "We can at least throw it into recycling."

With a quick glance around, he added, "Some of this could be what you just left behind."

"Exactly," she agreed.

With one final look, he walked out. She followed; they closed the doors, and, after checking that the other apartment was locked, they proceeded to dump the garbage bag into the bin. Carrying her suitcase, he led the way down the back stairs and outside. At the rear door he stopped and just let his senses fill in.

"What are you doing?" she murmured just behind him.

"Looking for danger."

"But your senses?"

"I'm at about halfway," he admitted, "which is bad because it's enough that I think that I can use them, but it's not enough that I'll know of any blind spots."

"Well, I can tell you that it doesn't look like anybody is out here."

"But, if it were you out there somewhere," he noted, "and you were trying to completely terminate a whole group of people, wouldn't you keep up surveillance?"

"Not if I was cocky enough to assume I had already hit everybody."

"I got the impression that Mera was hit before you. Do you think so?"

"Yes. So maybe our hitman assumed that, having got her, he also got me."

"We need to find Wilson."

"Agreed." She looked over at his ride. "You ready to make a go to the truck?"

He smiled at her. "You saw me arrive, didn't you?"

"I've been staring outside all day, trying to figure out what my next move was. I didn't recognize the truck, but you're pretty hard to hide."

"I guess," he agreed, "even though that's bad news too. I was so worried about you that I bolted straight here, instead of putting on a disguise."

"Well, you changed your walk and the way you hold yourself," she noted, "but I've worked with you for three, four years now. So fooling me is a different story." Not to mention her heart recognized him right away.

Back at the truck, he turned on the engine. "Do you have an address for Wilson?"

She shook her head. "I don't."

"I had one on file, but I don't know if it's any good anymore."

"He lived on Rue Borda, didn't he?"

He nodded. And they headed out.

"Why are we even still in Paris?" She rubbed her forehead. "I should have just left."

"And yet you were working right up until five o'clock yesterday, right? Or two days ago, I guess."

She nodded. "And?"

"When would you have left?"

"The next day, so yesterday!" At that he nodded. "Meaning?" she asked.

"You were shot at that night. The only way you would have been safe was if you had booked flights out of the country right after work."

"So …" It took her a moment, and then she continued that thought in a low voice. "They really didn't plan on us leaving, did they?"

"No," he replied quietly, "I don't think they did."

"Or it was meant to look that way, but it wasn't our government who did this."

"And I would love to think that, but, with all the communication taken down, we have no way of finding out."

"Right. That's a problem too. What if our bosses were also hit?"

He shot her a look, as he pulled out and turned a corner. "Now that hadn't occurred to me."

"It is a possibility though, right?" she murmured.

"Well, we'll have to wait until we get secure lines to find out because we can't take a chance of anybody else tracking us."

"I get it, but what if they're in trouble?"

"They have support."

"Which is something we don't, right? Got it." She shook her head. "I really don't like the sound of that. We've always had money, flights, equipment, whatever we needed. We've always been able to call and have it ready and available for us."

"Yeah, and that is past tense." He looked at her. "Now we're on our own."

She looked at him. "You do remember that I don't work for them anymore, right?"

"Meaning?"

She hesitated, and he continued. "I don't either. Remember? None of us do."

"What do you mean by that?"

"What do you mean?" he challenged.

She frowned. "I guess what I'm trying to say is that I don't want to be involved. I don't want anything to do with this." She raised both hands in frustration. "I thought I was retiring. I thought I would be out of this before I headed back stateside and could get a new life."

"What's the matter with Paris?" he asked, with a lopsided grin.

"A lot if it's not secure," she argued. "We don't have the protection of the government anymore. If anything goes wrong, we're the ones who go to jail."

"Yes," he agreed, "that's very true. Chances are we would have had some protection before, but we couldn't have guaranteed that. After all, we never got into that kind of trouble. Or … never got caught anyway."

"So what now? Do you think we'll never get into trouble?" she asked.

"I gather you want to go back stateside? Leave Paris? Leave this nightmare behind?"

"Of course I do," she stated. "I've got friends and family there, and so do you."

"Well, I don't have any family. Plus we might end up in

England."

She nodded at that. "In a way, that would make sense. You have connections with some of those people."

"Well, we had connections through work," he corrected.

"Yes, but, after time, they become almost personal."

"Almost, yes, but we also don't know if we've gotten the kibosh worldwide either. So far, nobody knows we're alive and functioning still."

"And that's the thing, you're not fully functioning! And, without that, we have no team. We have no skills. We have no backup, no assets. We have nothing."

He shot her a hard glance. "We were all special ops before we joined this team. We still have skills, the same as everybody else."

"Great, but it always felt a whole lot better having that extra advantage."

Damon laughed, one of the first free sounds she'd heard from him. "I get it. I really do. And I agree it was a huge advantage to do some of the stuff that we did. But I sure as hell won't roll over and show my belly just because some of my abilities have been hit."

"Sure, but you're one in seven."

"Eight," he corrected.

"Fine, one in eight. But still it's far from the same thing. Without the support of the government, we're screwed."

"And what if it's deliberate on the part of the government?"

"Well, then we're doubly screwed," she cried out, "because they will track us down."

"How would they do that?"

"Because they have as many resources as we had, plus they have the finances. We don't have squat."

"We have the finances." He smiled. "Absolutely no problem there."

She looked at him in surprise. "Meaning, we can still get equipment and things that we need?"

"Absolutely."

"Oh." She settled back then, pondering it.

"Does that change things?"

"Well, it helps," she agreed cautiously. "Does it change things? I'm not so sure. Because if we're really being hunted by our own people, there's really no place to hide."

"No, but do you think that everybody will be okay with us being hunted?"

"If they thought we were a danger, yes," she noted quietly. "And there was talk about shutting us down for a long time because they were uncertain how stable you guys were."

"I know that we weren't privy to all those conversations, but we were certainly privy to their fear."

She snorted at that. "Didn't seem to matter what we said. They were always thinking that you guys would go off the deep end and blow up something."

"Which is probably why we ended up getting shut down, but I don't know where they got that idea from and have to wonder if somebody was feeding it to them."

"Well, it wasn't me. You guys are the strongest individuals I've ever met. There was nothing even the slightest bit haywire about you."

"Well, thanks for that, but a word of warning. You can bet that Terk isn't feeling anywhere near as nice or as congenial as you might have thought he was before."

"Of course not. He's being hunted and the team attacked. And, if it is by one of our own, he'll go underground and find out who did this. If his skills are intact, that would be something. He was the strongest of you all."

"Exactly." Damon smiled in satisfaction. "I'm glad you understand."

"Is that the game then, retaliation?" She hoped not.

He shook his head. "No, it's not retaliation. It's about survival. If we don't solve this, we'll never have a life. It's one thing for those of us who are alive and able to go underground and to hide for the rest of our lives, but it's an entirely different thing if you and Mera have to."

"Meaning, I'm not as good at it?" She watched as he drove the truck around a corner.

"You're not as good at it," he confirmed. "It's not what you three are."

"And yet it seems like whoever it was considered us enough of a threat that we had to be taken out too. Whoever is doing this—and, as much as I can't quite accept that it is our own bosses, but because of the timing it's likely—it could have been instigated by some other party."

"But remember this. What was done to the team had to have been done by another team like us."

She sucked in her breath. "I didn't consider that, and that's scary."

"It is, and it also means that something much more powerful and more dangerous than us is out there. That's what we don't want."

"No, of course not," she agreed. "Every country wants to know that they have the most powerful weapon."

He laughed. "Isn't that the truth."

As they drove toward Wilson's address, she spoke. "I would really hate for that to be the final answer. I don't want to look over my shoulder for the rest of my life. It's hard enough to sleep now."

"It doesn't look like you've slept at all," he murmured.

"Oh, so now you're telling me that I look like shit too, *huh*?" But a note of laughter was in her voice.

He tossed her a grin. "I would never say that, but you look like you didn't get much sleep last night."

"Well, when you wake up, and seconds later your bed is riddled with bullets, it does tend to make for more sleepless nights."

"Of course. Don't you want to stop that?"

"I do, of course, but you're asking for a commitment that's very dangerous for me."

"Yeah, but how is it more dangerous than what you've already been through and what you will face in the future when they figure out you got away? … We're here with you."

She struggled to answer that. She was terrified to leave and be alone, and she was terrified to stay.

"Let's go check on Wilson."

DAMON AND TASHA pulled up outside what looked like a series of small flats. Checking the apartment number on his phone, Damon hopped out with her, and they walked across the street. He opened up his senses, knowing that again he would only get half the information and would get slammed with pain as soon as he tried to increase it by much. He opened up and checked. And frowned in surprise. "Absolutely nothing is around here." He paused. "Almost like a deadness is here."

"That's not good." Her footsteps slowed.

He grabbed her arm, dragging her closer to walk right

beside him. "Not necessarily," he noted quietly. "It feels more like they've been here and gone."

"Of course they've been here and gone." And then she sucked in her breath. "But been here and gone where?"

"Come on. Let's go find out."

They walked up and knocked on the door at Wilson's flat number. When they got no answer, Damon turned his back on the hallway. "Keep watch." Then he took out his tools and popped the lock.

"The fact that it's locked, shouldn't that be a good indication?"

As he went in, he checked the lock inside. "No, you can lock it and then still close the door from the outside." He lifted his nose and froze. "You don't want to be in here."

She looked at him in surprise. "Why not?" And then she caught the smell. Her eyes widened, and she bolted from him. "Wilson," she cried out, and she raced around the flat, heading to the bedroom. As soon as she got to the open doorway, Damon was just a hair behind her.

And she stopped in the doorway and cried out. "Oh my God, oh my God, oh my God!"

He snatched her into his arms and pulled her back, so that she wouldn't see, while Damon studied the layout and the inside of the room. "Looks like Wilson was first."

She started to cry in his arms, as he held her close.

He carefully analyzed the scene. Same MO as the others. Just random destruction in the living room, but the bed had been shot up, and unfortunately Wilson had been sleeping.

Damon walked her back to the living room, "Stay here. I need to take a closer look."

She nodded and didn't say anything, then sat down on the arm of the couch, her arms wrapped around her chest, weeping silently.

He was sorry to leave her alone, but, if ever they needed confirmation on details, it was right now. He headed back to the bedroom, pulled out his phone, and took photos. It looked like Wilson had taken three bullets, all direct hits. He probably hadn't even known what hit him.

Damon took more photos around the place, including the living room, which had been trashed to make it look like a robbery—if anybody was stupid enough to assume the bullet holes were a part of that. To Damon, this looked like an execution.

Shaking his head, Damon stepped back out again, and, dragging her with him, they exited, got into the vehicle, and he immediately started it up and pulled away. As soon as he could, he pulled off the road into a parking lot, surrounded by lots of other vehicles, and he called Terk, who answered on the first ring.

"What did you find?" Terk asked impatiently.

"They got him first. Wilson is dead, and it has all the looks of a professional hit. He's number one of all of us," he murmured. "He has been terminated."

CHAPTER 4

TASHA WATCHED CAREFULLY as Damon drove through the city, sliding into back roads, taking corners in a roundabout way, as he took them to their new location. She didn't even know what to think; she was half numb, half full of pain and sorrow, and terrified of what was coming. "I still can't believe somebody is trying to wipe out the entire team."

"It's hard to think otherwise." His voice was quiet inside the cab.

She shuddered and wrapped her arms around her chest. "It just seemed so unbelievable."

"Remember the work we do though." He quickly glanced in her direction.

She studied his profile. "The thing is, I always saw us as taking out bad guys. Not good guys taking us out."

His lips quirked. "We were," he corrected. "That's exactly what we were doing. But we would be naive to assume that some of these bad guys wouldn't try to get back at us for it."

"And I would understand that long before I would think that it was our own government," she murmured.

"And we can't know which way this will go yet," he argued. "We're waiting for status changes on all the rest of the team. Only Terk and I, at the moment, are capable of doing anything."

"And that's how I feel right now. With Wilson gone and Mera hurt, there's just me. And how is it that I survived?"

"I think he was either short on time, or—because it was the third one, and he'd done the first two successfully—he just assumed he'd hit his intended target, made a quick dash out of your place, and disappeared. He did three in one evening, so timing was an issue."

"I guess that makes sense."

He nodded. "It's one thing to go in and kill somebody, cross your tracks to make sure you're safe, and nobody knows it was you. It's another thing to hit three in one night," he stated. "That takes a pro."

She shuddered at the thought. "Like the pros we were?"

"Like the pros we *are*," he corrected. "And, no, it wasn't any of our team."

She frowned at that. "I never thought that," she protested.

He shot her a hard glance. "Good, I'm glad to hear that because our team is down, and I doubt they could have done that to themselves."

"We were supposed to get a couple new recruits before they suddenly closed the department. Do we know anything about them?"

She watched his eyebrows shoot up, as he contemplated her suggestion. "No, I don't. When they decided abruptly to shut us down," he murmured, "I don't even know what happened to those two. I presume they were told not to show up. I'm not sure they were anything other than a red herring to keep us thinking everything was trucking along like normal. They didn't arrive though."

"No, they were due to come in two weeks, I think," she

replied. "But what do I know? It seems like everything was happening around me, and I was completely oblivious."

"Not oblivious, just doing your job, focused on the here and now. None of us could have known this attack was coming."

"And yet I feel like we should have," she noted. "Who else does this kind of work without knowing something like this is coming toward them? That inside edge should have warned Terk of that upcoming danger. So why didn't it?"

"It was very well planned," he admitted. "We were all taken out within a twenty-four-hour period, likely within a few hours of each other."

"And that's scary too because it takes a pro team to co-ordinate something like that," she murmured. "A team that's skilled and has resources behind them."

"Which is why I was wondering if it was another government. Personally I'm considering Iran."

"Because of what happened on the last mission over there?"

"Well, it certainly is a possibility, isn't it?"

"It could be somebody else," she agreed, "but it would take the right people."

"We've been targeting the right people for a couple years now." He slid her a glance. "And you know them yourself."

"I do." Her mind raced, as she thought about all the different cases. "But so often, we've gone after kidnap victims or coups that were happening or taking out terrorists on the sly," she murmured.

"And all of them have teams," he muttered.

"Right, I just didn't think of it." She paused. "I never considered a significant attempt at retaliation. Over the years it never happened, so I thought we were safe. Plus we were better than everyone else," she stated, with a caustic tone.

He frowned. "It's not that we were better than anyone," he argued, "but you're only as good as your team, or, when we were running individual ops, we knew we only had ourselves to depend on and, therefore, cut all ties to anyone else. When we came back with the job done, nobody knew what we had done, where we'd done it, or how, and that was a good way to operate."

"Is that what it's come down to now? Each of us alone?"

He shook his head. "No, I need Terk, and he needs us."

"And I'm not sure I need either of you." There, she'd said it. Clear, crisp, and completely based on fear. He didn't look at her and didn't even acknowledge her words. "What? You won't even say anything?"

"I know where you're coming from," he replied. "I'm hoping that you will agree to help us."

"And why would I?"

At that, he gave half a snort. "You weren't an ostrich at any point in time in the last several years. But, right now, if you think that sticking your head in the sand will help your situation, you're wrong."

Glumly she stared out the window. "Meaning that, as soon as they realize I'm alive, they'll come back after me?"

"I would."

She sucked in her breath. That statement said so much. Because whoever was out there who attacked them was just as cold and proficient as the team she had worked for. But it was so much easier to work for her team when she thought that they were the guys on the winning side. The good guys. She sank back into her seat, then closed her eyes and tried to let the fear inside calm down. But it was hard, damn hard. "What if they never found out?" she murmured.

"You'll spend the rest of your life looking over your shoulder. And, when you least expect it, they'll be there. You won't feel the bullet in the middle of the night. Just like Wilson didn't."

She stayed quiet for the rest of the trip.

When he stopped going around in circles and darted into the back alley of what looked like a large storage compound, full of warehouses, her eyebrows shot up. "Is this what you're calling offices these days?"

He shot her a look. "It's temporary."

She pinched her lips together. And, when he pulled up in front of one, then hopped out and unlocked a door at the side, she followed him.

"What about my stuff?" she murmured.

"Leave it there. We're not set up for sleeping here."

She stepped inside and realized it was literally a huge warehouse, with completely concrete walls. "Do you think the concrete in here is enough?"

"It's not steel reinforced, so no," he replied briskly. "But it was a temporary solution for a time we didn't really want to consider."

"No," she agreed. "We were disbanding, not trying to set up a new headquarters somewhere else."

He nodded. "Exactly."

When the door opened at the back of the warehouse, she jumped, startled, and then walked in Terk. He took one look at her, and she saw the fatigue and the worry clearly on his face. She raced toward him, and, just before she reached him, his arms opened up and wrapped around her. He held her close, gently rubbing her back.

"I'm so glad they missed you," he murmured.

She felt the tears in her eyes. Something was so damn

strong and so … almost stalwart about Terk. Everybody had had their own particular qualities, but something extra was about Terk as a leader. He was the most compassionate and empathetic man whom she'd ever met. Yet he could be as hard and as cold as ice, when the situation dictated. But he always paid a high price. And unfortunately she'd seen that time and time again. When she finally stepped back, she brushed the tears from her eyes. "Mera is alive, but she's terrified."

He nodded. "Who isn't?"

She winced at that. "I was hoping you would tell me that it was all fine and that you already had it all well in hand."

He gave a bark of laughter. "I would if I could, but it's not quite so simple."

"No," she murmured, "it isn't." She looked around. "I see boxes upon boxes."

"Yes." He nodded. "New equipment."

"What kind of equipment?" she asked, walking over and studying the contents. She saw new computers with actual hard drives, extra bits and pieces in open boxes, and monitors.

"Can you set this up?" Terk asked.

She nodded. "I absolutely can, but that doesn't mean it has any place to go. Particularly in a place like this. We had special satellite feeds running through the steel and the concrete to get the communications that we needed. Otherwise we would never have gotten signals in or out."

He nodded. "I know, and this is only temporary here, so it's a matter of doing what we can."

"Got it," she noted. "Let me get started then." She started opening up the rest of the boxes. She looked around and saw a couple folding tables off to the side. She walked over, set one of them on its feet, and started unpacking the electronics. This was her field, no doubt, but she did worry about it. "Does anybody know we're here?" she tossed out. When a sudden silence came from behind her, she pivoted and looked at the two men, both staring at her. "Please tell me that's a no?"

Terk shook his head. "Nobody knows, at least not this location."

"But do some people know we're alive?"

He nodded slowly.

Her eyebrows shot up. "Is that safe?"

"We have to trust somebody, and I've chosen to trust my brother," he replied coolly.

She stared at him for a long moment. "I didn't even know you had one."

His lips quirked. "Not only do I have a brother but he's a twin."

"Holy shit." She stared at him. "How did you ever hide that?"

"I didn't even try to. My brother was also working in the US Navy for a long time. Now he works for a private security company."

She wasn't sure she liked the sound of that. She studied him carefully. "Is it safe? Because, even though he might believe in his company, that doesn't mean that everybody in his company believes in him."

"And that's a very good observation," Terk noted, "and I appreciate the concern, but, in this case, I do trust him *and* the company."

She shook her head. "A lot of people are in companies." She hesitated. "You can't trust all of them."

"I get that," he noted. "And, if you want to walk, you

can at any time."

She frowned. "I don't have any place to go, and you know it."

"Then trust me, just like you've trusted me all these years."

She let out a slow deep breath. "It's not that easy."

"No, it isn't," he agreed, "and, right now, I guess trusting me is probably even harder than normal because we somehow ended up in this situation."

"Yes, but I can't blame that on you."

"Why not? I do."

She shook her head. "No, that's not on you. We were disbanded. We were supposed to be gone, and you were heading off." She frowned. "Oh, you were going to Texas."

He nodded. "Exactly."

"Something about …" And then her face cleared. "Your brother. You were going to see your brother, weren't you?"

"Yes, I just never made it that clear."

"No, and I wasn't really reading between the lines because I was more focused on finishing off what we had to finish off."

At that, from behind her, Damon asked Terk, "Any update on Celia?"

"Not at the moment." Terk chewed his bottom lip.

Damon suggested, "Maybe it's time to check in."

"I would like to," Terk agreed, "but I'm not getting any answer from the compound."

"Ouch," Damon replied. "That's not cool."

She pointed at the tables. "Give me a minute and I'll set it up. Are we talking about Legendary Security out of Texas?"

He nodded.

"Your brother works for them," she realized slowly.

"Yes, is that a problem?"

"No, but we've used them for various things over the years."

"We've used them when I needed help," Terk agreed, "or if we needed something special that they had access to."

"I didn't know it was your brother though."

"That's because I didn't advertise it. That's probably a good thing, or he'd be dead right now."

She stiffened. "Have you checked? Is there any chance that they've been targeted too?"

"Well, they have been targeted," he confirmed. "And in a way that you won't like. And since I don't know the status of any of it right now"—he shrugged—"I just have to let it lie and to trust in them."

"We don't do trust well," she noted.

He gave a bark of laughter. "I thought that was my line."

She felt a reluctant amusement tugging at her lips. "No, you're right, but I'd feel better if you got an update from them."

"I was just about to. I spoke to my brother earlier, but we got cut off. I haven't been able to connect since." Just then his phone rang. He pulled it up, looked at it. "That's him now."

"Put it on Speaker," she ordered.

He raised an eyebrow and studied her.

She nodded. "We're all in this now. Let's not have any secrets, half-truths, or partial information come between us. There's just the three of us for now, so let's see who we can trust, who we can use, and who we can't."

He gave a quick nod. "Merk?"

"Yeah, it's me. Jesus, bro, when you bring it on, you

bring it on."

"Is she alive?" he asked urgently.

"You have no freaking idea."

TERK SHIFTED THE phone. "I'm putting it on Speaker."

Ice spoke up. "Terk, we've got her. She's sedated."

"Is that safe?"

"It's likely the only answer at the moment. She has been traumatized and tortured, but that isn't affecting the baby's health at this point, though the mother's in rough shape. We got the C-4 off her without any trouble by cutting the signals, and we took down two men. Unfortunately," she added, her voice hard, "the men self-terminated before we could question them."

"How did they do that?"

"Capsules in the mouth," she snapped. "And believe me. I'm pissed about that. I really wanted a live body to question." Just enough emphasis was in her voice that nobody had any doubt about the *questioning* part.

"Levi, you there?"

"Right here, Terk. What's up?"

"We had three operatives who handled our communications. One is dead. One has been shot and is more or less out of the game. At the moment we're trying to keep her secure, but she's not cooperating. The third is here in the office with us."

"Who died?" Merk asked.

"Wilson."

"Shit, so you've got the two females left?"

"If you're talking about me," Tasha spoke up, "I'm here.

Mera has been shot, and she's definitely worried about having any further involvement in this or with us."

"Does she realize that her life is on the line?"

"She does now, but, as of a couple hours ago, she still wasn't sure whom to trust. Having someone shoot up your bed in the middle of the night has a way of doing that. Trust me. We're both lucky to be alive. She caught two bullets, so she feels even more vulnerable. It'll take her a bit to come in from the cold."

Levi asked, "What can we do to help?"

"I need a communication assist," she replied. "I'm just starting to set up equipment, so it'll take me probably two hours, and then I'll need a satellite."

"You got it. I'll patch you through to Stone. As soon as you are ready, he'll help you set up everything." Levi hesitated and then asked, "Can you do it on your own?"

"With Stone's help on the other end, for sure," she answered, with a note of humor. "We've worked together many times."

Just then Stone walked into the room and spoke, "Hey, Tasha. I'm here. Let me know when you're ready to go. Do you have a phone?"

"Not of my own, no. I borrowed Damon's earlier."

"We have burner phones," Damon explained. "I've got a box of them here somewhere. She'll call you when we find them."

"Good enough."

Terk stepped up to the phone. "So seriously, how is Celia?"

"Is that her name?"

He hesitated. "I think so."

"Think so?"

"Remember. We're not operating at full power—" he replied, but Merk interrupted.

"Brother, even injured or without your senses, you're still more than 120 percent of anybody out there," he argued. "Do not doubt yourself."

"It's not so much doubt as it's walking through a fog," he explained. "It's like losing your sight and being temporarily blinded. Those special senses were a part of me. Something I used almost every moment of the day, without even realizing it because it was so natural. How badly is she hurt, Ice?"

"Couple busted ribs, broken wrist, her shin is cracked, and some muscle damage, but she walked here on her own, which is freaking crazy. She is sedated, but she's in danger, needs to be hospitalized at a level beyond the facilities we have here."

"Please keep her there if you can," he replied immediately. "I know you can do this."

"Maybe," Ice replied, "but, if she stays under for too long and goes into a coma, I'll have trouble pulling her back."

"I suspect she will go into a coma," he said quietly. "And I can't really explain or tell you how or why."

"Terk, if you have information on how to keep her alive, you need to tell me," Ice demanded in a harsh voice. "This isn't the time for holding back. If something has happened or had been done to her that's out of the ordinary, then it would really help to know."

"I don't know," he added for emphasis, "*anything*. And I'll tell you if I do." And, with that, he hung up.

ICE LOOKED AT Merk, as he stared down at the phone. She asked him, "Jesus, what the hell is going on?"

"His team has been targeted," Merk noted, "and, of course, we know what that's like. He's walking in the dark, but, in this case, for him, the dark is all-encompassing."

"And that's the problem with having an extra sight like that," Ice replied. "Somebody knew it. Somebody targeted it, and somebody took it out."

"I'm not sure they took it out." Merk lifted his head slowly to look at the rest of Levi's team gathered here. Something far off was in his view. "It's possible that Terk's gifts have been muted, diffused in some way, like walking behind glass, or not at full strength. But something in his voice I didn't quite get."

"I heard it too." Ice stood, her legs akimbo, a military stance, in stark contrast to her extended belly. She then crossed her arms and glared at him. "Next time he calls, see if you can get an update from Terk on Celia. Like a confirmation that's her name for a start."

"It's what he called her. But he doesn't know a last name."

She froze at that. "She's pregnant with his baby but he said he never met her. How is that for a mind bender."

"Sure, but remember who you're talking about." Merk gave her a lopsided grin. "My brother *meets*"—and he put that word in air quotes—"a lot of people in a lot of ways, and none of it is physical."

She groaned. "You know what? I would much rather deal with somebody who's a threat right in front of me than with all these ghostly supernatural aspects. Your brother is damn scary. He's part of our team and part of our family, but at times I look at him and wonder just where the hell he's coming from because he's got information that none of us could ever even begin to access."

"Yeah." Merk stood. "What do you think it was like growing up with him?"

She shook her head. "More power to you that you didn't drop him to the floor at some point in time."

He burst out laughing. "He is still my brother."

She grinned. "I know. That's why it's safe to say it to you because you know where I'm coming from. He is sure a fascinating person, and we need to help him all we can."

At that, Stone filled up a huge mug and walked over to the sideboard, his hands wafting in the air, as if struggling to make a choice from all the offerings.

Merk looked at him and suggested, "Don't even hold back. You'll have a long day."

At that, he nodded, then grabbed a plate and took two cinnamon buns and a handful of cookies. "You're right. I'll need something to keep me going." He flashed a grin at the others. "If you need me, you know where I am." And, with that, he headed upstairs to wait for the call from Tasha.

Merk looked at Ice. "How bad is Celia?"

"She's bad, and it's not so much the physical injuries. They will heal. I've done the x-rays, and I'm checking to see if we'll have to bring in a surgeon to do something to help straighten up the broken bones. I've sent them off to my dad for another look, but, if everything comes back clear, then she just needs time to heal, physically and emotionally."

"And the baby, are you sure he's okay?"

"*He?*"

Merk flushed. "Slip of the tongue."

But her gaze narrowed on him. "I don't know the sex of the child, and I'm not doing any test to find that out. It hasn't popped up in anything yet," she stated, "so make sure it was a slip of the tongue."

"Got it," he replied immediately.

She shook her head. "Damn, things just went sideways in a big way."

"No, they went sideways forty-eight hours ago," Levi corrected, "but now it's up to us to stop the slide."

"So how do we keep Terk's team safe?" she asked. "They're over there. I wish to hell they were here."

"And that is an option we have," Levi murmured.

"You never brought that up."

"Honestly I figured Terk would veto it immediately."

"He would," Merk agreed. "He'll want to do his utmost to make sure that he doesn't bring any more danger to anybody here."

"Yes, but that also leaves him alone in the cold."

"Which, as you well know, is not a bad place to be."

She groaned. "I get it."

"Ice, go take care of those you can," Levi ordered, with a gentle grin.

She rolled her eyes at him. "Terk is family."

"He is, and we will do everything we can to make sure he's safe." She frowned at him, but he wouldn't have anything to do with it. "Go. You're getting too involved."

"How can I get *too* involved?" she snapped.

"Because you care," he stated. "We all care too, but we'll keep our heads on this one."

"Don't you tell me that I won't keep my head," she argued.

He walked over, dropped his forehead to hers. "Please, just go get some rest."

She sighed. "Fine, but, when I come back, you guys better have a plan of action, or else I'm stepping in, and I'll create one." And, with that, she stormed off.

Levi looked over at Merk. "Now do you want to tell me what that slip of the tongue was all about?"

"No, I really don't." He stared back at Levi.

"And *was* it a slip of the tongue?" Levi asked.

"As far as I know, it was," he replied. "Believe me. Growing up with Terk was a very unnerving experience. I protected him as much as I could, until he got control of his abilities, but it wasn't easy to have your brother look into your mind and see where your thoughts were all the time."

"No, I imagine it wasn't. Are you sure that you don't have the same ability?"

"Absolutely. No way I have the same ability. You think I wouldn't have used it all these years that we've worked together if I could have?"

Levi frowned at that. "That is the most telling part. Absolutely you would have. If there were any bad guys to hunt down, and you had hidden weapons, you would have used them in a heartbeat."

"Thank you," he said. "Believe me. You're not the first one to doubt me when it comes to this, and that has made my life a whole lot different. Even my brother didn't understand why I don't have the same abilities, and he wanted me to, especially as twins. We were identical, except for that part, and I was jealous for a long time. Then I began to see just how twisted and difficult it made his life, but, even then, I still wanted to be special, like he was." He shook his head. "It definitely took us some time to sort through that."

"If you even got through it on your own," Levi added, "you're doing well. Your brother is tortured and yet incredibly talented."

Merk smiled. "That he is. He's also a really good man, and we have to help him."

"That's in the works, and anything they need, we'll come up with, and that includes a safe place."

"What do we have for locations in Paris? Or are you thinking maybe England? They'll need to move fast, whenever they have to," Merk noted, "and it's only a matter of time before things go sideways there again."

"You know what? He really needs a steel building and thick concrete, but something I've never really understood," he added, "is how he needs that level of barrier to stay safe and to make sure no one can access anything, yet he can still get through all that to use his skills."

"He's created some psychic tunnel, and I can't even begin to understand it," Merk admitted. "But it's his way of getting in and out of cover."

"Sometimes I think we've been playing undercover agents for way too long," Levi noted. "Because, honest to God, when did some of this bizarre stuff start sounding normal?"

Merk laughed. "See? You'll come along with us on this crazy-ass ride regardless," he noted. "That's just how it starts."

"And I get it," Levi agreed. "It'll be harder for Ice though because she wants so badly to keep him safe."

"Ice wants to keep the world safe," Merk noted, "and giving birth herself hasn't helped that."

"No, it hasn't."

"And having another child won't stop that protective mother feeling either. Did you tell her that you know yet?"

Levi looked at him. "What do you mean?"

"That you already know the sex of your child."

"How is it I'm supposed to know?" Levi asked, his gaze boring into him. "When she doesn't?"

Merk smiled. "You already know you have a second son coming," he stated. "A matched set – at least according to Terk."

"Hell no, I don't know that, and she's really hoping for a girl."

"And you?"

"I don't care, as long as it's healthy."

Merk nodded. "Well, Ice will be happy with a healthy baby boy."

And, with that, Levi turned and walked out.

Merk stared down at the phone, sent his brother a text—a warning to watch his back—and then Merk walked over to the sideboard and grabbed a coffee. It would be a hell of a long day. But, if he could do anything to help Stone set up things for his brother, then Merk was on it.

With that, he walked up to the control room.

CHAPTER 5

TASHA THOUGHT IT would take a couple hours, but instead it took six, and she still had multiple laptops upgrading drivers, downloading software, with the physical security setup ongoing. But, at that point, all three of them were working on it, with Stone and Merk on the other end. By the time she sat back at her "desk" and looked around to see what else had to be done, she couldn't even remember the last time she had eaten.

"I need food," she announced, then looked over at the others. "What are we doing about things like that—and sleep?"

The two men looked at each other, then over at her. "We need to find a place for the night."

"You don't have one?" she asked in surprise.

"No, it was more important to focus on setting this up."

"I get that," she noted, "but, short of me crashing in the corner, I'll need some rejuvenating rest, and before that I need food." She got up and walked to the door.

"Wait." Damon was two steps behind her.

She turned, looked at him. "What?" She'd be the first to admit that she got angry whenever she got hungry. "I need food, and I mean it."

"I get it." He held up his hands. "I'll drive you wherever we need to go, and we'll bring back enough for all of us."

"Fine, but we need it fast."

He opened the rear warehouse side door, which she didn't even realize was locked. Then she stepped out to see complete darkness all around her. "Jesus, we've been working all day? No wonder I'm starving."

"Pretty much," he agreed, "but also a hell of a storm is moving in." They got into his truck, and he asked, "What kind of food are you looking for?"

"Something substantial," she said in a curt tone, "and definitely something with carbs."

"Pasta?"

She hemmed and hawed at that. "That could work, but I'll also need meat to go with it."

At that, he burst out laughing. "So, just lots of everything."

She grinned. "That would help. You know what? Even a grocery store, where we could buy some French bread, maybe some salamis and cheeses. A selection of easy-to-eat finger food like that wouldn't be a bad idea to just keep around."

"We can do both," he suggested. "This isn't something that we want to come out for on a daily basis."

"So both then," she stated, "but I don't really know where to go. I don't know what's safe anymore." And then she looked at him and frowned. "Did you change the color of your hair? When the hell did you do that?"

"Yeah, not enough color to really *change it*, change it. Just enough to make you question it."

"*Huh*, I didn't even notice."

"You were a little busy."

She nodded. "That I was, and that's why I'm so damn tired and cranky right now."

"It's all right. We're getting food."

And, with that, he took a couple corners, drove down a main street, and pulled off to a small area, where she saw a grocery store up around the corner. "Are we walking?"

"I'm just waiting to see if we're being followed."

That silenced her. She sat back and waited quietly, the gloominess growing inside the vehicle. When he turned the engine back on again, she asked, "Does that mean yes or no?"

"It's clear."

"Good, we'll need more trackers then because we need to keep track of all of us."

"Yes, and that's something that we haven't had to do up until now because it was something Terk could do."

"Can he still?"

"I don't know. We'll need to ask him. We also have another shipment of security gear coming in tomorrow."

"Fine." She yawned.

He drove closer to the grocery store; it was small and still open but wouldn't have anything terribly fresh, and that was not something she particularly liked. "I'd rather hit a bakery first thing in the morning and get fresh bread, if that's a choice," she muttered.

"There's got to be some benefits to being in France. We'll pick up a few things here," he suggested. "I've got a coffeemaker somewhere in the back of the truck that I didn't even think to pull out."

She stared at him indignantly. "You mean that I could have been sucking back on coffee this whole time?"

He grinned. "You could have, yes, my bad. Totally my fault."

"Wow, I assumed you didn't have anything like that yet,

so it never occurred to me to ask."

"And you assumed wrong," he stated, "so maybe it really is your fault after all."

She snorted at that. "In your dreams." She hopped out and, with him at her side, wandered through the store, picking up a few things.

"We'll hit a bigger grocery store later."

There were a few croissants, though perhaps a little stale, but she was hungry. She picked up a couple.

Damon asked, "Are you sure?"

She nodded. "We're not done working tonight, and I need food."

"We can pick up lots of fresh stuff at the other stop we have to make."

"Have you already ordered it?"

"I have."

She put the croissants back, grabbed milk, some coffee, some cream, and a pack of cookies, then wandered around and picked up some cheese, then put it back.

"Again in the morning?" he asked, a question in his tone.

She nodded. "I still prefer good food."

"Fine."

With that, they paid for what they had and hopped back into the truck. As they pulled out of the small parking lot, she asked, "Do you think the other food is ready?"

"It should be," he muttered.

They pulled into the next place, which was a small restaurant. He disappeared, leaving her in the truck. She sank down below the window, so she couldn't be seen as she waited, but was in danger of falling asleep as soon as she closed her eyes. She wasn't kidding that she needed food.

Mostly to keep herself functioning when it came to times like this. It was all she could do to keep plowing forward if she didn't get sustenance.

She often wondered if she had blood sugar issues when she needed food this badly; otherwise she got the shakes. But she hadn't had the time or the real desire to put forth the effort to get it checked out. She wasn't too worried about it right now either. No guarantee she would live until morning anyway. At the attempted dry humor she opened her eyes and watched as Damon walked back out of the restaurant, checking around the area, even as he walked toward her.

He hopped in. "It's all good. We can go now."

She smelled the pasta inside the huge carry-out box that he had. "Did you order enough?"

"I would think so," he replied, "particularly if we're coming out in the morning."

"Yeah, but who's coming out in the morning?" she asked. "You don't want to do this too often."

"Nope, but we can make an exception for tomorrow because we still have to pick up a delivery."

"Ah, well, that makes sense. How early is it coming in?"

"Should be first thing."

She nodded. "A couple good bakeries are around here. We need to hit them."

"We'll also need meat and cheese," he reminded her. "And maybe some fruit."

"I'll make a list." Immediately She brought out her phone, opened up a note, and started typing in things that she needed to get. By the time she was done, they were already back at the warehouse. She hopped out and grabbed the groceries they had picked up.

He carried in the takeout, and she followed him into the

warehouse. As they entered, they found Terk standing in the middle, his eyes closed, his hands outward at his side.

"Terk, you okay?" she called out. There was no answer. Frowning, she walked closer.

However, Damon grabbed her arm. "Remember. Don't touch."

She nodded. "I just want to make sure he's okay."

At that, Terk opened his eyes and stared at her directly.

She made a small shriek and stepped back. "God, I hate it when you do that," she cried out.

He cracked a smile. "How do you think I feel when people step into my space?"

She glared at him. "I was just checking to make sure you were okay."

"That is the only reason you're still standing too," he replied in a mild tone.

She raised her hands, palms up. "You always were touchy about that."

"What? That I don't like people stepping into my space? Yes, I am," he muttered. He sniffed the air around him. "Food."

"Yeah, that was hard to figure out, wasn't it?" she asked, a wide-eyed look in his direction. And then she smiled. "Come on. We need to eat. We're all crashing pretty fast."

"That's actually what I was doing," he muttered.

"What? Crashing?" she asked.

"Ha, ha. No, recharging."

"Well, if you can recharge like that," she noted, "you're better than the rest of us."

He nodded. "I probably am."

She rolled her eyes, and then was immediately distracted by the smell of the food, as Damon pulled it from the bag.

She didn't know what it was, but it looked like lasagna, heavy with meat and cheese. "Oh my God."

He served up three portions onto paper plates that they had picked up at the grocery store and handed one to her.

She grabbed a fork and sat down, and then, holding the plate in her hand, she ate several bites, trying to slow herself down so she didn't just shovel it in. But that was hard because it was so good, and it was at the perfect eating temperature, a little on the hot side, hitting the spot like so little could.

She looked around when she emptied her plate. "I'll need to crash soon too."

They nodded and pointed off to the other corner, where the boxes were stacked, and she noted an outdoor camping mat and a blanket. "*Great*, not exactly what I was hoping for."

"No, but for the moment," Damon explained, "it's the best answer."

"Says you," she muttered. She headed to the washroom, assessing whether she'd had enough to eat or if hunger would wake her up in the middle of the night. By the time she decided she was probably good to go, she headed back out. "I need at least an hour."

"You've got several," Damon stated. "Go grab whatever sleep you can get, while we finish setting up this stuff."

She hesitated. "Are you sure you don't need me?"

"If we do, we'll wake you," Terk replied.

The thing is, she knew he would, and trusting that was how this evening would play out, she crashed on the temporary bedding and closed her eyes. She heard them behind her, talking in a normal tone of voice about the security. She wanted to disconnect from it all, but it was hard.

When the phone rang again, she half listened and half didn't. It was Merk again on the other end, but she couldn't hear all the conversation. Just as she was deciding if she should give it up or not, she felt sleep crashing in on her, and she slowly closed her eyes and went out.

DAMON WALKED OVER to check on Tasha. At least this time she was finally out cold. That was good because she was one of those people who worked hard and then crashed hard, as if somebody had literally just pulled the plug. It was a fascinating thing to watch, and something that he himself had cultivated as a skill for when he was out on missions. But he didn't see very many other people doing it themselves, and it was his first opportunity to see it working on someone else. It was kind of freaky.

When he walked back over, Terk looked up and asked, "Any change?"

His friend shook his head. "She's still out cold."

"And that's probably the best way for her to be." Terk added, "They did get x-rays on Celia, and Ice's father agrees that she's fine without surgery, but she'll need time to recuperate. Well, that's probably the best-case scenario because she's safe where she is, with Levi."

"How safe can they be?" Damon asked, looking over at Terk.

"They're on high alert, fully aware that she was sent to them on purpose."

"And why would they do that?"

"A message. That I can get to you, wherever you are,

anytime, and all of those around you. I didn't even know she was important, and here she was, already tortured and a captive."

"But it's not your fault," Damon stated. "You didn't know them. Hell, you didn't even know Celia." He looked closely at Terk's face for confirmation.

Terk shook his head. "I don't know her."

"Did you ever do a sperm donation?"

He winced. "Yeah, don't worry. I already thought of that, but I didn't do anything formal."

"So, … you want to tell me how they got your sperm?"

He glared at him. "I've been racking my brain, trying to figure that out."

"Sex with somebody who might have done something funky to keep it alive right away?" Damon asked, trying to make it a little more delicately understood.

Terk snorted at that. "You know that I've kept myself separated from all relationships."

"That doesn't mean you didn't hire somebody for an hour," he suggested. "Nobody would blame you."

"I would blame myself," he said. "Things have been in a shithole for a while."

"I know you felt that way because you couldn't resolve a couple cases in the best way possible and then this issue with the bosses. You can't control others."

"We've done so well," he noted, "and I fought so hard to keep the department open. I thought we were good and then *boom*. We're not good."

"What are the chances that they told you that they were fighting for you, but they were really just pushing the timeline so they could shut you down?"

"That's exactly what they did." He stood, stretched, rotated his head and neck. "The only thing I can think of, and I really hate the thought, is on the one mission about nine months ago," he explained, "when I was injured."

"And?"

"Remember? I was put into private nursing care for a few months, until I recovered."

"Months? I think that was only a few weeks."

"Well, it felt like months. Anything that kept me off work felt like an eternity."

"And you're thinking that maybe that's when your sperm was harvested?"

Terk tested that phrase out in his mind and realized this was probably what had been done to him. "I don't know what else it could have been," he stated. "Aside from being knocked out cold when I didn't know about it at another time, that's the only time I can think of that somebody could have gotten their hands on me. You know what? I almost had a vasectomy when I was younger because I didn't want children." He shrugged. "And now to think that a child of mine is growing in a strange woman's belly, who probably had no choice in the matter either, that is some kind of freaky."

"You think she was inseminated?"

"Well, let's just say, I didn't do the job." He frowned. "I mean it. I have never met her before in my life."

"What if she looked differently?" he asked in an odd tone.

"You mean, like they changed her appearance, or she did? Like maybe she was working for somebody and was the person they utilized for this? I don't know. I don't know what else to say." He paused. "I don't remember her, but I can also tell you that, on an energy level, I don't know this woman."

"Ah, that's a completely different story then, isn't it? God, what the hell does that actually mean then?"

"I don't know," Terk muttered quietly. "But it's pretty damn frustrating to think that this is what my life and my offspring has come down to. Already my child, nonexistent in most people's minds at this stage, is being held hostage by some asshole with a plan all his own."

And, for the first time, Damon could see the absolute fury among the intense emotions rolling through his friend, as he verbalized what he thought had happened.

"That—" Damon stopped. There were no words to describe how something like that could even feel. He knew perfectly well about Terk's attempt to have a vasectomy when he was younger because he didn't want to procreate, didn't want to add anybody else to his family who could then be used against him. "How likely is it that somebody knew that's how you felt?" Damon asked quietly.

Terk looked at him sharply. "What do you mean?"

"Well, that's a huge issue for you, right? I mean, that's why you wanted the vasectomy, and that's why you were so disciplined to make sure to never leave any offspring anywhere around the world," he murmured, "because you felt so strongly about it. What if this was done deliberately because somebody knew that's how you felt?"

At that, Terk crashed into the chair closest to him. "God, that would be like having actually created this with my thoughts."

"Well, I wasn't quite considering that," Damon said, "and I know that anybody in this type of work knows perfectly well that keeping your thoughts open and contained and within a positive force was damn important in order to keep a balance and to keep an eye on everything churning around them."

Damon stood and paced around the room. "It's just a thought that came to me when you were so adamant about not having done this—that the one thing happening is the thing you worked so hard to prevent. It doesn't seem coincidental, you know? Do we even know if this woman wanted a child?"

"Who knows?" he replied absentmindedly. "It would come down to whether she believed that this was an absent anonymous donor or if she had any idea that she's already been inseminated or if she thinks it's her boyfriend's child or something."

"How can you be sure it's yours?"

At that, Terk just looked at him.

"Ah, so you've already connected with the baby then?"

"Enough to know it's my energy. It's my connection, and I can see the child in my head."

"And?"

"It's a boy," he noted. "There's something different about it though, that I don't quite get."

"*Huh.* Well, when we come to something like this, how could you? I'm not sure that either of us or anybody else has had any experience connecting with unborn children. Have you ever even heard of such a thing?"

"No, and I wouldn't have thought it possible, except that I'm living proof that it is," he muttered quietly. "I just can't believe I'm in this situation."

"I know, and that's why I'm wondering if it was deliberate."

"Well, it's definitely deliberate," he confirmed, "but I hadn't considered that I would be personally targeted in such a way."

"No, of course not." Hearing an odd sound, Damon got up and walked over to check on Tasha. When he realized the blanket had slipped off her shoulder, he quickly pulled it up and tucked it around her. Then he tiptoed back and away again.

"It's still there, isn't it?"

Damon looked at Terk in surprise. "What's still there?"

But that flat stare wasn't something Damon could ever really walk away from, so he shrugged and nodded. "Apparently. It damn near killed me when I saw the inside of her apartment and thought she might have died."

"I still don't like that the three of them were all targeted just because of their association to us."

"I know," he murmured. "And we have nobody to even take care of Wilson's body."

"No, but an anonymous tip was given to the police, so they should have taken care of that by now."

"Yeah, we've used that trick a time or two, haven't we?"

"We'll have do it more than we would like in the future too," Terk murmured. "We'll need more support, or we'll be in trouble."

"What about your brother and Levi?"

"Well, they're helping us right now, and, like I said, they're on lockdown themselves over there. They are also trying to backtrack the two guys and Celia's movements, which is just as important. Still no success in that area yet though."

"Absolutely it is important," he agreed. "All of it is important right now because, if we mess up on one front, they'll come around and get us on another."

"We've already seen that." Terk shot him a hard glance. "They aren't leaving any loose ends behind. Any screwups will have permanent consequences."

CHAPTER 6

TASHA LAY HERE quietly, hearing some of the conversation rolling over her head in bits and pieces, before she dropped off and woke up again to some of the conversation still continuing. The Celia secret blew away Tasha. It absolutely stunned her that somebody would go so far as to torture Terk by doing something like producing a child of his without his knowledge. How can anyone do this to another human being? To a pair of human beings? And yet, from some of the psychos whom she'd seen out in the world, it shouldn't surprise her.

She had been part of an effort they had worked on to take down a large child pornography ring. Not exactly the type of stuff they were used to doing, but Terk had brought the case into the office, and they'd all been more than eager to help. And they had succeeded, rescuing some forty-seven children, the youngest of which was just a few months old. Even now Tasha got sick just thinking about it.

But the cases that needed trimming back were those dealing with assassinations of government figures and various world leaders around the globe. She had never been called to weigh in on those decisions; the admins just did the job given to them to do. And now that she was more intimately involved with the decision-making part of this team, it felt weird, though right in some ways, because it seemed like a natural progression—as long as she forgot entirely about the part in between, where she had been targeted, where Mera had been shot, and where Wilson had been terminated.

And she still hadn't had a chance to even begin to grieve for Wilson. He was a quiet, intense young man, who had visions of a better world, visions that would no longer come to pass for him. It broke her heart to even think about him being cut down as a loose end to be trimmed, like excess fat.

As for Mera, Tasha understood not knowing whom to trust, not wanting to get involved. The fear driving through Mera was powerful and, in her case, was coupled with the pain and anxiety from being shot. But taking control of that fear and doing something positive with it was worth so much; otherwise you sat in that same victim state, expecting to be attacked. And one of those times when you turned around, you probably really would be.

Tasha hadn't known it at the time, but her decision to work here, to actively do something to take charge against those who had attacked her, had proven to be very empowering.

She hesitated and then rolled her head to the guys. "Any food left?" She sat up slowly, as Damon walked over and stood there, staring down at her. "I'm fine, you know." She gave him a wan smile.

"Good, glad to hear that, but you don't look it."

"I was just thinking about Mera and Wilson," she explained sadly.

"And I get that, but the thing to be more concerned about now is ourselves."

"I know. I know, but—" Then she stopped. "I guess there really are no *buts*."

"We don't have time for *buts*."

"I get that. I just think it's sad that Wilson was cut down with no sign of remorse. He seemed to be the first of the three of us, and somebody was just focused on shooting him and moving on to targets two and three."

"What you need to remember is that, no matter what level these guys are on, they don't care—not about us, not about anything except their end goal, whatever that may be."

"What levels are you talking about?" she asked.

"Whether the big boss man at the top of the pyramid or one of the local hired guns on the bottom."

"And what is that end goal anyway?" She had heard the guys discussing their theories, so this question was mostly rhetorical.

Slowly she stood, accepting his offer of help; then she brushed off her legs and shook them out, easing up the kinks from lying on the hard surface. She stretched, moving her arms and torso up and down and from side to side. "God, that won't do me for very long," she muttered, pointing to the pallet on the floor. "I know you guys have the training for this, but I don't. I can sit in a chair for a whole lot longer than I can lie down on that type of mattress."

"We should have beds by tomorrow night," he murmured.

She rolled her eyes at that. "How will that be any improvement if we're still in here?"

"Well, that's not the plan. We're looking for a safe home base."

"Then we shouldn't have set this up here."

Damon turned toward Terk, but he was *unplugged* for the moment. "This is temporary. And we will set it up all over again."

She shot him a look, knowing he wasn't telling her everything. "I get that it'll probably be much safer and faster to set up a second time, but it still feels like a waste right now." She immediately walked over to the table, where the food was still sitting out. "We need to get a fridge." She sniffed the air. "Coffee?"

"Terk made some." Damon grinned. "I didn't really connect it at the time, but he must have known you were waking up and put on a fresh pot."

She nodded and looked over where Terk was, sitting cross-legged in a corner. "What's he doing? Recharging?" The fact that he could do that just blew her away, but she'd seen him do it time and time again.

"Yep, we'll always have one on patrol."

"Oh, in that case, he's down, and I'm up, so you can go down."

"I plan on it, but I wanted to check in with you first."

"I'm fine." She gave him a wave of her hand. "Go on. It's all good."

"You sure?" He hesitated.

She nodded. "I'm very sure."

She watched as he headed to where she had just gotten up from, then crashed, pulling the blanket up over his shoulders. Satisfied that he would stay down, she went over to the coffeemaker and poured herself a cup. Over half a pot sat here, waiting for her, something that she was really grateful for.

As she stood here, sipping her coffee, she studied how much they had done. She checked the to-do list on the pad of paper. All the top items she had left had been crossed off, and they'd added three more things to the bottom. She studied them, realized what they were, and nodded happily. "Wow." She sat down and started setting up log-ins. "This is great."

She was almost back to feeling like she had the world at her fingertips. She checked in on a couple of her emails, even though she no longer had government access. Then she thought about it and wondered further. She checked her log-ins, the old ones, but they were defunct. She'd always kept all the log-ins for all the team members in her head, just in case somebody got shut down, and she needed to bring them back online. She quickly ran through them all, testing to see if they were inactive too. Only Wilson's was active.

She frowned at that, immediately changed the password, and logged in. From there, she set up a new persona and routed it through Africa. She wasn't exactly sure she should be doing this, but she needed a way to get government data access via the back door. And this was one of the few ways to do it. From there, she logged back in through that persona and headed over to a couple colleagues who she knew stateside. Checking that they were still around, she then logged out and logged back in as them. And then she smiled.

"Good enough." She noted that she was in under their names. One was off on sick leave for a few months, which was interesting, probably from an accident, and that meant using that email would trigger an alert. Tasha frowned at that, then headed over to the admin side and set up a brand new one. She quickly filled in the back history, having done this time and time again when Terk's team needed to create fake backgrounds.

She set it up using a different name, then picked a picture off a stock photo site, set that up, and proceeded to erase her tracks, sending the email off for this new person to set up her own account. Having filled that out, she went back in, set up a password, then made it all incognito and shut it down.

With that complete, she walked over to a different computer, brought it up, and checked that she could log in. With that done, she headed back to the first machine and completely wiped it of her most recent activity. Then she logged in under the newest persona, checked that nobody was watching or tracking her movements, and set up a few more safeguards, so she could access it from any location without them tracking her back. And logged out.

By the time she had done that, she was pouring a second cup of coffee. She thought about all the other databases that she needed to have secure access to.

She frowned at that, then headed back into the one database, tricked the computer system into seeing her as an admin, and gave herself access to multiple databases. She couldn't go too high up into data protected by serious security clearances, otherwise the government would become suspicious. But, if she had access to everything she'd already been used to, that was a different story. It didn't take long before she was sitting once again, feeling like everything was good.

Beside her, Terk opened his eyes, looked at her, and asked, "Did you get in?"

Surprised, she looked at him and slowly nodded.

"Did you erase all your tracks?"

She nodded again. "Yep, and added extra safeguards." She smiled. "I do know what I'm doing."

He smiled at her. "I'm glad to hear that because we have to trust you right now."

"Not a problem. Now go back to sleep so I can get to work."

With that, he closed his eyes, and she leaned forward

and started the hunt.

DAMON STUDIED THE boxes with joy.

"We've got a lot of work to do," Tasha said.

He nodded. "And it's work I love." He rubbed his hands together. "I'll get started in here, unpacking the security gear."

She nodded. "Make sure you guys have new trackers on, so I can code them and can keep track of where you are at all times."

"Yeah, as soon as we get them unpacked." Damon looked over at Terk. "Is this everything?"

"It should be. According to Merk, it was all delivered."

"And you didn't even see your brother." She stared at him. "How can you stand that?"

"Because I love my brother," he stated, "and keeping him away from me right now keeps him alive. That's the most important thing." And, with that, he turned and walked to the other room.

She looked over at Damon. "I guess I said the wrong thing again, *huh*?"

"You never say the wrong thing. Terk won't take it the wrong way. He'll always appreciate honesty over anything else."

She pondered that as they started opening the boxes. "I just don't want to upset everybody. We're all on edge right now."

"We are," he agreed, "and the sooner we get answers, the better off we'll all be."

"Answers are good, but answers don't track down people," she argued, "and you can't go alone."

He looked over at her, and she saw the hard glint on his face. "Just watch me." He didn't mean to be quite so fierce and realized he was when he saw the fear that moved across her face. He tried to give her a brighter smile. "Don't worry about it, Tash," he murmured. "Just know we'll hunt down whoever did this."

She nodded slowly. "I'll need information on Celia from Terk, so I can track why everybody has gone to his brother."

"I wondered if you would notice that." He smirked. "I've started some searches, but we really don't have a whole lot to go on."

"No, but I now have equipment, and we can't keep letting Terk ignore this."

"He's a little resistant to it. He has always kept his family private, and, of course, in this case, it's more family and far more complicated."

She nodded. "I know." She hesitated and then said, "I'll go talk to him."

As she darted past, Damon wanted to stop her, but, if they would all be working together, they had to figure out how to communicate. He heard their voices, but they weren't raised, so that was good. He set about opening up all the boxes and doing an inventory to ensure they had received everything they'd asked for. He found the shelving, which he quickly put up, and then started setting out the equipment they needed to work each day, plus the physical security systems. But he still needed to find the cache of weapons. Only a couple more boxes to go. Had they been delivered as well? He would love it if that were the case. By the time he got through the last few boxes, he was overjoyed and grinning like a small boy.

Handguns, a couple semiautomatics, a stash of grenades, lots of artillery, lots of related ammo. He whistled when he got to the last case and found it full—a long-range rifle, with silencer, scope, the whole works. He lifted it up, placed it on his shoulder, and grinned. "Now we're talking," he said. "Now we're talking."

Of course they still needed some more wheels so they weren't seen in the same vehicle, plus simple things, like hair dye. He'd done his hair, but he wasn't so sure that Tasha would be up for the same. When she walked back into the room a little bit later, he looked over at her and asked, "Well?"

"He was pretty reasonable," she replied. "So we've set up some database searches, looking for anything. Celia is still unconscious, so she hasn't been able to tell anybody anything. Levi's team did a forensic check of her, but they found not so much as her fingerprints on file anywhere."

"Of course not," Damon noted. "These guys are pros."

"Would they really blow her up? An innocent woman in all this?"

"For these guys, I wouldn't discount it as their plan B. However, we can't assume she's innocent," he reminded her.

Tasha winced. "I feel like she's probably very similar to what Wilson was."

"You mean, roadkill?"

She gasped, and her face paled at the thought.

He winced, rubbing his face, wondering at his own stupidity. "I'm sorry. I didn't mean it to be quite so harsh."

"Well, it sounds like it *is* that harsh," she agreed, "but you're right. It is roadkill. I just feel bad for her. The same as for Mera. I wish I could talk to her, but I don't think she wants anything to do with any of us. And I can't really blame her," Tasha said, teary-eyed. "We were never that close, but I thought we were closer than this. I thought that, when the chips were down, we'd pull together."

"But she's the one who's injured, not you," he murmured. "And sometimes, when people are hurt, they just want to hide away until they feel better. I wouldn't be at all surprised if she makes contact down the road, asking what she can do to help."

Tasha brightened at the thought. "That would really be great if she did."

"It would, and we could use the help, couldn't we?" he asked, with a grin.

She turned and looked around in amazement at the work he'd already done. "You've been busy. I didn't think I was gone all that long."

"Most of this stuff just needed to be pulled out of the boxes and placed on shelves. I figure, once it's all on display, we can organize it better and figure out what we've got."

"Did we get everything as ordered? That is the next question."

"I think so, but I don't know what he asked for."

She laughed. "You guys didn't work out the supply list?"

"Not even sure Terk handed over a supply list. I think he probably just asked them to set us up, loaded for bear."

"And this is what that looks like, is that it?"

"I presume so," he said cheerfully. "We have lots of ammunition now. At least we can defend ourselves here."

She stared at him in surprise. "Anything small that I could keep?"

"Yes." He walked over. "I thought about you when these came in." He pointed out a pair of small pistols. "You like these in particular, don't you?"

She smiled and nodded. She picked up one and hefted the weight in her hand. "This looks about right."

"There's also an ankle holster and a shoulder holster that should work with those weapons." He quickly fitted her with both and asked, "How does that feel?"

"It's good," she said in surprise. "Are we wearing these all the time?" He looked at her, as she winced. "Stupid question. Of course we are."

She loaded the small handgun in her shoulder holster, then bent down and fitted the even smaller one at her ankle, pulling down her pant leg to cover it. "I have a little bit of clothing with me but not a whole lot."

"You've got more than we do," he said. "I think that last bag there is clothes from Merk. I'm hoping something in there will fit me too."

"Well, you're about the same size as Terk," she noted, "so I wouldn't be surprised." At that, she walked over, pulled up the bag, and found that, indeed, it was full of clothing. She unpacked it and laid it out on the table. "Looks like six sets here," she said. "So three each?"

Terk walked in from the other side. "That was the plan. If we need more, they'll get us more, but this was an initial order to have for right now."

"And they were fast," she noted in surprise.

"Yeah, that's Levi's company, everything at their fingertips, including information."

"Good. In that case, do they know who did this to us?" she joked.

"They're on it." Damon's voice was dead serious. "When they know something, they'll tell us."

She looked over at him, her eyebrows raised. "Seriously? They too are hunting down whoever attacked us?"

"Of course," he replied. "We need all the help we can get, and that's the only group Terk and I can trust at the moment."

"Good." She nodded. "If you trust them, I guess I will too. I know I wasn't terribly supportive of the idea earlier, but we can't do this alone."

"No"—his voice went quiet—"we can't, so let's be grateful we have the help that we do."

They exchanged glances in surprise because a camaraderie was here that Damon didn't feel they had had between them until now.

Damon asked Tasha, "You're quite comfortable with him, aren't you?"

"Of course. We've been working together for a while."

Damon nodded slowly. "You and I have been too."

"Yeah, but Terk wasn't giving me the major brush-off like you were."

He stared at her as she walked past him. "Was it that obvious?"

"Sure it was, and, for the longest time, I wondered what the hell was eating at you. I finally figured out it was your problem, not mine," she said blissfully.

He burst out laughing. "Nice to have so much self-confidence that you didn't think you had anything to do with it."

"Oh, I figured I had a lot to do with it, but only so much I could do *about* it. That was your problem, and you would have to solve it, one way or another. I did talk to Terk at one time, saying I wasn't sure I could be part of the team because of you."

Damon stared at her in shock.

She nodded. "I mean, everybody talks about teamwork,

and yet, with you, I felt like I was completely shut out."

He slowly sank into the chair. "Good God. I had no idea."

"Nope, I figured you didn't." She smiled. "But Terk told me that you had some issues to work through and promised that it had nothing to do with me. So I trusted him then, and, well, I'm trusting him again now," she said. "I couldn't understand what the hell your problem was."

"Sorry, I was trying hard to keep the family together." He raised his hands in surrender. "I'm not sure you know how I felt."

"Which is ridiculous," she muttered. "For a supersmart guy, you were really stupid."

And, with that, she turned and walked away.

CHAPTER 7

O N THE OTHER side of the warehouse Tasha chuckled softly, trying to keep the noise down, because she could see Terk was off in the corner doing something. Unsure what, and not wanting to disturb him, she sat down at a computer to check on the information she'd been running. She printed off the list of license plates, only to realize something.

She walked back to Damon, took one look at his, then smiled. "So, we have a little bit of information. The vehicles seen outside Wilson's and Mera's were stolen."

"Of course they were." Damon shook his head. "What about at your place?"

"Still no sign of anything abnormal," she murmured. "But, while I'm not sure what to expect, it seems unlikely they would change their pattern at that point."

"Any personnel movements back at home base?"

"Two promotions and one person quit. I don't know that you know any of them," she said. "I'll print it off for you."

"Are you keeping track that closely?"

"Damn right I am," she stated, with a fierceness that surprised her. "Somebody did this to us. I kind of liked the idea of it being our boss, but I really don't like the idea, if you know what I mean."

"I get it," he agreed, "but it still comes back to the fact that we probably know too much."

"They didn't have to do it this way," she murmured. "We've been loyal the whole time."

"And we can't jump to conclusions," he reminded her.

She rolled her eyes at that. "Of course not," she muttered, "but it's okay for everybody else to?"

"Nope, it sure isn't," he said. "But hold your horses, we're getting somewhere."

She grabbed the printout with the names of those who had shifted within the department. He looked at them, frowned, "I don't know any of these people."

"I even printed off the faces in case that made a difference." She handed him a new set of paperwork.

He looked at it, shrugged. "Nope, nobody I know."

"So, whether that's good or bad, I don't know," she continued, "but those are the changes this week for our bosses. Well, in the entire department," she corrected. "So maybe nobody is doing anything right now."

"I rather imagine they're in panic mode, trying to figure out what the hell is going on."

"Do you think they even know?" she asked Damon.

"They don't have bodies, so their panic is escalating," Terk said from the doorway, his hands on his hips, studying Tasha. "In which case, they'll be trying to contact us. Yet they're the ones who shut everything down. So I'm not sure how much communicating they'll do."

"Do we want to reach out?" she asked quietly.

He shook his head. "No, we don't. I'm waiting for them to reach out first."

"Will they though?"

"Yeah, eventually they'll get desperate enough and probably contact Levi."

"Why do you think they'll contact your brother's boss?"

He gave her a hard grin. "Anybody in the industry who knows we are twins will know that my brother and I are close, and, if anybody will know anything, it'll be him."

"Well, in that case, they'll be tracking his phone lines and checking all communications, trying to find you through him then."

"Absolutely," he agreed cheerfully. "We're working out a way to trap them."

"If somebody shows up here, are *you* planning on"—she stopped, winced—"are you planning on talking to them?"

"Wouldn't that be a good idea?" Terk studied her face. "Is that a problem for you?"

"Well, the trouble is, if you talk to them, they'll tell everybody that they saw you, *alive*," she said quietly. "And that's something we can't have happen."

"Nope, we can't," he murmured. "Whether there's a connection to the US government or not, somebody out there knows something, and they'll do whatever the hell they can to get the rest of the information they need. And that includes taking down our own men. So, whether we're protecting our old group or we're protecting just ourselves, talking to these others means finding a permanent solution afterward."

"I don't want everybody killed," she said instantly.

"Neither do I," Terk agreed. "As a matter of fact, I don't want anybody killed. That includes our own people. Do you have a suggestion on how to handle that?"

"I don't know," she cried out in frustration, "but there has to be another answer than murder."

"Is it murder?"

"Of course it's murder," she declared. "They're our team too. Well, used to be our government team. We can't just go and kill everybody because we want answers."

He smiled. "No we can't, but you also have to consider that, if they know we're alive, it just launches round two of the assassination of our team."

"In that case, it becomes self-defense, and that's a different story. But we'll not just go around killing anybody." She caught the glint of laughter in Terk's gaze. "You were just testing me, weren't you?"

"You're a very fierce personality," he muttered. "I just wanted to see what side you truly were on."

"You mean *trust?*"

"No, not at all," he corrected. "I already trust you, but I also know, in these circumstances, honor and ethics can go out the window in a heartbeat. And I had to know which way you were leaning."

"I'm leaning to keep everybody alive," she clarified, "and, barring our ability to do that, I want to make sure that it's only the bad guys who die."

"Good. And now I need to go recharge." He glanced over at the other room. "I'll go see if I can get one of the beds set up." Then he turned and walked away.

She stared after him, wondering at the wisdom of even being here at all. When she'd first joined the group some four or so years ago, she had wondered about her own sanity, at being in this group at all. She also knew that the kind of work she did was what had gotten her in a hell of a lot of trouble already, and this was almost a way of making atonement for it. But she wasn't so sure that it was the best idea right now.

She could just cut and run. Who the hell would follow

her? It's not like she knew anything. But then she thought about all that she could do, all she could access to get whatever she needed, when she needed it, just because of the skills that she had gained, and she realized that she would be very valuable to some people. Or very dangerous. Hence the recent gunman in her life. And that meant she was here, whether she liked it or not.

As she returned to her computer, Damon stepped up closer and asked, "You okay?"

She nodded. "Yeah, I am. It's just a hard decision to realize that there really is no decision. This is where we're at, and I can hardly leave and expect to stay safe by myself." She felt something inside her almost want to break down and cry. "But it's really not what I expected for my life."

"If we would have had any inkling that this was coming, it would be a different story. We feel responsible for Wilson's death."

She nodded. "And we did check that he's really dead, right? You didn't have a case of missing persons or anything else?"

"No, I thought of that at the time because we've dealt with duplicitous deaths before," he shared, "but I'm the one who checked his body, and it was definitely him."

"No cosmetic surgery to make him look different, nothing?"

"No, it was Wilson. I'm sorry."

She replied with a watery smile. "Well, it was a bit much to hope for."

"The thing is," he continued, "if it was that, then we'd know for a fact that he was one of the bad guys, or set up to take the fall for the bad guys, and then we would have to take him down—at least question him first."

"I know," she replied. "So maybe it's better that he's dead. Because I don't want to face anybody who we know in this and find out they've betrayed us."

"Nobody is comfortable with that." His voice was firm. "This isn't something you ever get comfortable with, but maybe, in this case, it's a good thing it's not Wilson," he said. "I know you were sweet on him."

She looked at him in surprise. "Seriously?"

He nodded. "Weren't you?"

She sat up taller and frowned. "No. Hell no. He was a nice enough kid, but I wasn't sweet on him. If you had used the brains inside your head, you would have realized who I was interested in. But *that* you put a stop to."

"No I didn't. I was just trying to—" And he stopped. "Wait, seriously?"

"Yeah, but you didn't even know it back then."

"*Back then.* … So not now?"

"God, you're really pushing it, aren't you?" She sent him a look. "This is hardly the time or the place."

"You know that that was what got me into trouble the last time." He tilted his head. "Because, if I'd said something before, maybe we wouldn't have wasted all this time."

"Maybe." She shrugged. "And maybe it would have been worse. Maybe we would have come together only to find out we hated each other, and we would have a hell of a time trying to work together now."

He laughed. "I highly doubt it, but I get where you're coming from."

"Good, because I sure don't."

He stared at her in surprise.

She shook her head and sighed. "This is just all too big of a nightmare for me. I deal with details. I deal with the internet," she explained. "I can handle things that are in front of me, something concrete that I can see. I can follow the bytes. I can read the code. I can check changes in the code and detect patterns and anomalies. But the rest of this stuff? Wow, I don't know how you guys manage to do it."

"We do it because we have to, because we're good at it," he said, with a firm smile. "And, once you find something that you're good at, it's fun, right? Because you can make things happen. You can make the keyboard dance. You can make the code do what you want it to do. So you find out that you're really good at something, and you stick with it because it's incredibly rewarding to be good at something in your life."

"Did you ever wonder if you would be good at something?" she asked him quietly.

"All the time." He smiled. "All the time. Only as I ended up in this field did I realize what I'm really, really good at."

"And what is that?"

He lowered his voice and whispered, "Warfare."

And then the room fell silent.

IT WAS HARD to sleep; it really was. Damon dozed in and out, his mind constantly processing everything going on, and it was hard to still that activity. They'd almost established everything they needed to get functioning again, and all of it incognito, carefully concealed within a shell company that nobody could easily track. Sure, people like him would get there eventually, but it would take them some time.

Hopefully this would give Merk's team enough time to find out what the hell was going on and to find those responsible. Damon still considered it likely that the US government was behind it all, but he also knew that Terk was focusing on Iran as well—and with good reason.

They'd come up against a team over there that had been damn near as good as them. They'd put the others out of business, but what if they only thought they had been put out of business, but it actually had been resurrected?

It was always a scary enough thought when you dropped a corrupt government that was killing off its own innocent people. There always seemed to be another government that looked better; yet, once they got into power, they became the same power-hungry greedy villains they had replaced.

And Damon felt like this secret op group out of Iran was similar. The fact that they may have some special abilities which he didn't understand was also terrifying. Because Damon now realized he and his team had been smug all these years, thinking they were the only ones. They had looked toward Russia as being another potential threat but hadn't really considered anybody else. Iran had blindsided them.

Terk's team had gone in and done the job and ran into the same kinds of obstacles that they usually presented to others. They had a great deal of difficulty getting past all the safeguards but had finally prevailed and had decimated the Iranian team. By the time Damon and the team had made it back home again—exhausted, beat, and, in some cases, severely injured—it had been deemed a triumph by the US government. But it had not been a great one for Terk's team because they'd seen themselves in the other group.

The Iranian team wasn't quite as developed, wasn't quite as strong, and sure as hell wasn't as effective, but they were on the same pathway. Damon knew his team had been struggling with the reality of that job ever since. They'd handed in all their reports and had done everything that they needed to do, but it had left a really ugly taste in their mouths. A taste that nothing could remove. And now they were left to wonder if they weren't getting some payback.

Damon hated to think so because that group had been using their abilities to wipe out top CEOs, transfer money, then doing arms deals, buying nuclear weapons, and completely annihilating small villages, as they took over any land they wanted. Terk's team was nothing like that. With a shake of his head, he abandoned his bed early in the morning and got down to work.

Damon sat here at his makeshift desk in their temporary headquarters, hidden away, wondering what he was doing and whether it was doing any good at all. He'd always been a firm believer in operating for the government for the sake of keeping the American people safe, and now he had to wonder if he hadn't become a liability and if the American government was trying to keep the American people safe from him. A sobering thought.

He slowly sat up, stretched a bit, used the facilities, and then came back. The coffee was long gone, and Tasha was still pounding away on a keyboard, as he had come to expect. She was damn good. A hacker, a team hacker at that, she had even had a hacker boyfriend going through high school. He'd gotten caught and done time—a lot of time, for stealing money from banks—while she'd been far more interested in hacking into the game systems that she'd been working on at the time, trying to figure out how the gaming community was using certain code to make things happen.

While her boyfriend had gone to jail, she'd been given a slap on the wrist, and the government had recruited her.

She'd laughed at them, thinking using her skills for the government would be the last thing she'd be interested in. Unfortunately, around the same time, her parents had been killed by a bomb planted in the family car. Immediately she realized that she had no way of knowing if it was intended to kill her too or as a way to punish her. She didn't know if it was because of the work she had been doing—or, more likely, that of her boyfriend—and her name had been linked to his after all.

She only knew that she was in danger, and it could quite possibly be from other countries because her boyfriend hadn't been particular or choosy about which banks or countries he stole money from. It wasn't like she had any of the money though. It had all been forfeited, the bank accounts seized. And, at nineteen years old, she'd become a somewhat reluctant employee of the government. A government hacker. She was talented and had risen quickly but was definitely known as nonconformist. She didn't fit into the office routine or handle authority well. She was a maverick.

Damon smiled at that because he knew mavericks. He knew a whole black ops group of them, and he had to admit that she would definitely fit in. No females were in that group to date, and, call him sexist, but, when it came to the type of work he did, it was harder for him to see a woman go out there and get herself slaughtered. And considering Tasha's strengths were computers and technology and software code, he figured she was right where she needed to be. And he was damn glad to have her.

"Stop staring at me," she said crossly. "You know I hate that."

"Are you sure you're not psychic?" he muttered, as he set about making a fresh pot of coffee.

"I don't have to be psychic to feel those laser beams in my back. You always were like that."

"No, I wasn't," he protested.

"Yes, you were. You were always watching me, studying everything I did. Did you think I didn't know you didn't trust me? Well, I did because you made it crystal clear. And now you really don't trust me all over again."

He froze at that. "Jesus, is that what you thought?"

She twisted around and shot him a hard look. "What else was I supposed to think?"

He flushed slightly at that because, of course, it was something completely different. He'd just been waiting for the group to disband and for the jobs to be over, before approaching her on a personal level. They worked well on a business level, but anything that screwed that up would affect the entire team, so he'd avoided any personal relationship. He was even careful with teasing, not wanting her to think something that wasn't there. The fact of the matter was, it *was* there, and only now did he find out that she'd been thinking the opposite.

She turned her gaze back to the computer.

"Don't you go blind watching that?"

"Nope," she snapped. "Do you go blind staring down a sniper rifle?"

"Nope."

"Right, so you do you, and I'll do me."

"And never the twain shall meet, *huh*?" he asked sarcastically.

She didn't answer but gave a shrug.

He'd often thought that something was between them, definitely a rapport, which he'd worked hard to keep on a business level. Maybe that had been a mistake. If ever there was a time to find a bond between them, it was now because he had to trust her and, if he didn't have that trust—well, he didn't want to think about it.

He walked over, sat beside her. "Listen. I always trusted you."

She looked at him again, but her gaze was hard to read. "Really? You were ever barely even friendly."

"I was friendly. We joked all the time."

"*Sure*, … and, at the same time, we didn't. It never went any further than that."

He winced. "That's because I was always trying to keep our relationship professional. Anything personal tends to upset the apple cart, and it was so necessary that the team be in sync that I couldn't do that."

"*Right*."

He heard the disbelief in her voice. He groaned. "I was planning on contacting you as soon as we were disbanded to see about going out for dinner."

He watched as her fingers stumbled on the keyboard, before she quickly corrected her mistake and tore right back through whatever the hell it was that she was doing.

"*Uh-huh*," she said, definitely a noncommittal answer.

He groaned. "I'm serious."

She just nodded.

"You don't believe me, do you?"

"There's never been the slightest sign of you being interested at all," she stated. "You've always been standoffish and difficult."

"Of course I was," he said, with a muted laugh. "How else was I supposed to keep my interest down and not have you aware?"

"What was wrong with me being aware?"

"Because the others would have noticed."

"Well, I highly doubt that anybody noticed anything," she replied curtly. "So, well-done."

"Ouch. I'm really not trying to be difficult over this."

"Well, you failed."

"You don't have to be so snappy either, you know?" he said. "Everything has changed now. It's critically important that we clear the air and trust each other … completely."

At that, she crashed her fingers down on the keyboard and then dropped them to her lap and glared at him. "But you don't trust me!"

He stopped, then hesitated. "You're wrong. I do trust you. Who I don't trust is me … around you."

That shut her up, and she just stared at him, her eyes wide.

He nodded and shrugged. "I've always been attracted to you, but it wasn't in anybody's best interest. It was never the right time. I tried to keep it all on the down-low, so you wouldn't know, and obviously I succeeded … too much."

She nodded. "You sure did. On my end, everybody else was friendly, but you weren't."

"I was friendly," he protested.

"Barely," she retorted. "You were civil. You were polite. You were all business."

He nodded. "Because I couldn't trust myself to be anything else."

She twisted again to stare at the monitors.

He hated that. He wanted to see what was in her eyes; he wanted to read her facial features, which was exactly why she had turned around. "I'm sorry," he said abruptly.

"For what?"

"For making you think I didn't care."

"Whatever." Then she let out a heavy sigh, reached up to rub her temples. "Why are you telling me all this now?"

"Because it's all about trust. It's about making sure that, if somebody needs us to do something, we can do it without an awkward relationship hindering us."

"I'm good if you are," she said.

"That's not exactly what I wanted to hear."

"I don't know what you want from me, Damon." She stared down at her hands in her lap.

He'd always loved her profile. She didn't look anything like the sharp-boned Mera. Tasha was young and soft looking, until you looked into her eyes, which were hard and seemed way too alive. When she'd first started back then, everybody had wondered what the hell they'd gotten as part of their team. But she had just sat down and gotten busy, taking control of all their electronics, and they'd been happy campers ever since.

"I'd like us to be friendly," he said.

She nodded. "I can do that."

"And maybe not quite so businesslike," he muttered, frowning. "Honest, I really was going to call you when it was over."

"I don't know what to say to that because I don't know if I would have answered."

He stared at her, his gaze boring through hers, wondering if it was a front. He could have sworn something was there. He had his own senses, but everything was only operating halfway. "You know we're all psychics on this team," he murmured.

"Not me," she snapped back, glaring at him.

"No, but you've got walls, walls that you have deliberately reinforced because you work with our team."

"Yeah," she said, with half a smirk. "Smart of me, huh?"

"So, maybe because you've been inside those walls, you can't actually feel what's happening outside."

That surprised her and lit her deep dark chocolate-brown gaze.

He nodded. "Just think about it. If you didn't have your walls up, maybe you would have been better at reading energy too."

"That's your domain, not mine."

"You know what I mean. You might have seen my intentions."

"Instead of it being the cold formality that you insisted on."

"And yet you know why," he stated.

"Nope, I don't," she murmured. "I definitely don't." But she wouldn't look him in the eye.

He reached over, grabbed her chin, turned it toward him. "Like hell." Then he leaned over and kissed her. A hard deep passionate kiss. Breaking it off, he stood and stepped away. "Coffee's done."

CHAPTER 8

A S KISSES WENT, it was just the tip of an iceberg. Yet Tasha felt the drugging power behind it. The passion, the need, all rolling in and yet forcibly contained. One thing about Damon that she had never misunderstood was the power within him. He walked with it. He was surrounded by it. He knew how to control it. The fact that he only had access to half of his abilities, which she knew included contacting others at a distance and finding them, meant he was more of a tracker than anything. She didn't understand how that worked because she was a tracker too; only she used bytes, not energy.

He was fascinating; he was deep; he was dark; and he was everything she'd ever wanted. But he'd made it very clear early on that he wasn't interested. So she'd thrown up walls to protect herself, hiding her feelings to make sure he never once found out how she felt. So his stunning statement now was something she simply didn't know how to deal with. Hope lit within her, but, at the same time, did she dare trust it? What did he want from her? And why now, after all this time?

It made sense, and she was a logical person, and everything that he had said rang true, but the circumstances had changed. But had they changed enough that he would actually think a relationship would be a good idea now?

Some of it felt off to her, and she wondered if he was just trying to lock her in so she would be part of the team again. She had to admit a part of her reacted with *Oh, hell no!* Part of her wanted to be long gone before this belated relationship went any further; yet she also wondered how she could walk away from Terk, who needed everybody on deck for this makeshift op, *and* Damon, whom she'd always been there for, keeping an eye on.

Whenever he was off on a mission, she kept tracking where he was, what he was doing, and how he was doing it, just to make sure he was safe. He'd had a few relationships, but she also knew they were more physical releases than anything. She'd done the same thing the first couple years after she joined the team but soon realized that absolutely nothing could come of it. She sought more than just the physical release, and the trouble was, these insignificant dates couldn't give more because they weren't the one person she wanted them to be, the one she couldn't have.

And now here he was, offering her so much more than what she'd ever expected, and she was dumbfounded.

Silently, she focused on her work, trying to continue working on the searches she was pursuing.

He approached her from behind. "Here's some coffee." Then placed a cup down beside her.

She looked at it, nodded. "Thank you."

"Think about what I said, okay? Going forward, the team will be whatever we make it," he murmured.

"What team?" she asked. "None of us have jobs. None of us are employed. We're on a vengeance trip. That's it." Of course what she wanted and what she would do were two different things because her whole life had flipped too. In a quiet tone, she added, "Let's just focus on the work."

"That's fine for now, and I agree it's what we need to do. But …"

At that, she ignored him because what else could she do? She watched out the corner of her eye, as he sat down with a list of things that needed to be done or ordered, and he started texting, she presumed to suppliers. She looked back over at him. "Is your phone secured?"

He nodded. "It is, and we'll change phones every day," he murmured. "Levi's team will send over supplies for us."

"That'll take a while," she warned.

"No, they'll source it all from here in Paris."

"So then it's probably the same suppliers that we've used."

"Maybe, but this way they won't know we are the ones who will be using them. We have to completely cut all ties with everyone we've used."

"Hence the shell company." She nodded.

"Yes. Exactly."

"So where do you want me to start?"

"I see you've been working on something. Why don't you bring me up to speed on that?"

She hesitated, and he waited calmly. "I was trying to track down the Iranian team from that mission, to see if I could find any sign that they are alive."

His eyebrows shot up. "Interesting. I was thinking the same thing, wondering if anybody was left. We were pretty sure there wasn't at the time."

"But that doesn't mean there wasn't a B team," she murmured. He glanced at her. "Just like there was talk about creating one here."

"That's true, but it's much harder to come up with more like us than you'd think."

"But the fact that there's already eight of you," she argued quietly, "means that there are others. You're not the only people in the world."

"No, I know that," he agreed. "Iran proved it. It's just a hard pill to swallow."

"Sure," she replied. "We were always of the opinion that we were the best of the best. But that won't wash right now, since somebody was able to attack and to take down our team."

"Something else I thought of. Can you start facial matching from any of the cameras around Wilson's place?"

"That's a good idea. I only tracked the vehicles so far." She was mad at herself for not having thought of it. "I'll see if I can get anybody the same from Mera's place and mine too. And, yeah," she added, with humor, "just to make sure that we're not being followed now. Where was the team when you were all taken out?"

"Different places, but all in the general area around our old Paris headquarters."

"In that case," she noted, "I'll start tracking out in that area too."

"You think that'll work?" he asked in surprise.

"I don't know." She shook her head. "What I do know is we have to find something that will work."

Cameras were all around the city, and she had them all linked up to her previous equipment, accessible under quick keystrokes, but she didn't have that available to her anymore. She would have to hunt them all down again. Swearing now that she hadn't done a backup, yet, even if she had, it still wouldn't have been available to her now, she got to work.

It was a good forty minutes later when she spoke again. "I can track the same person at Wilson's and Mera's, but I'm not seeing any sign of him at my place. And remember. We already knew the killers were using stolen vehicles."

"I went in through the back door of your place," he murmured.

She nodded. "And I don't have any camera access back there," she confirmed. "So I don't know what to say."

"Well, it is what it is. What about around the old headquarters?"

"Cameras were along the corner," she noted. "I picked up two suspicious vehicles, but then I lost track of them at the car parks." She pointed out on a map that he had laid out. "Depending on how many people they had with them, it might have been enough to have taken down the team. And then whoever went after all the admins on their own."

"Yeah." Damon nodded. "That's possible. We all had stayed behind, pretty unsure as to just what was going on in our own lives because the end had come so fast."

She nodded. "I know. I felt the same way."

"Which is one of the reasons I was going to contact you," he murmured, "but then everything happened at the end of the day that Friday. They hit us, knowing exactly when we were supposedly done, when everything would be locked down, cleared off, and cleaned out."

"We were the last tidbits to go."

He nodded. "That's how I feel this went down too. Can you get any license plates off those two suspicious vehicles?"

"I'll try." She brought up the cameras quickly, did a check on several, enlarging the photos as she went, looking for bits and pieces of license plates. "I can give you a few," she noted, "not that they'll help necessarily because I'm not sure the license plates were even valid, but I'm writing them down anyway." By the time she was done and had something printed off for him, she carried it over to the main table and asked, "Hey, what happened to the food?"

"Right, you wanted something fresh this morning, didn't you?"

She checked her watch. "It is eight o'clock in the morning."

"You want to do a run?"

"Yeah, besides, I need to move around a bit." She turned and looked at Terk to find his steady gaze staring back at her. She walked over and squatted down in front of him. "How are you doing?"

"I'm fine." He slowly rose and stretched.

"And the rest of the team?"

He gave her a ghost of a smile. "Holding."

"Is that what you were doing?"

"How did you know?" he asked, a quizzical glance her way.

"I haven't worked with you all this time without understanding *some* of what you can do," she murmured.

"What I can do and what I can do when I have strong receptive bodies is a totally different story," he explained. "I do have some of them on tap, but the other two in comas are not doing as well as I would hope."

She frowned at that. "Keep pouring that energy into them," she ordered.

He gave a slight low chuckle. "Yes, ma'am."

She shuddered. "Now that makes me seem old."

"Well, you're certainly old in spirit," he confirmed quietly. "You've come a long way since you started with us."

"It was such a shock," she acknowledged. "It's a long way from my teenage years and the hacking freedom that comes from being utterly unaware of the potential repercussions of your actions. I was young and stupid."

"And now?" Damon asked.

She shot him a hard look. "A whole lot older, a whole lot more experienced, and without a whole lot of trust left to give."

He winced and looked over at Terk, handing him a cup of coffee. "Have some coffee. We'll run out to the bakery. She wants bread and cheese."

Terk smiled. "Sounds good. I'm starving. I've been through a lot of energy, so make sure we have lots of protein."

"There's still leftovers from last night, some deli meats," she replied. "Everything is over on that table there. You know that we'll have to find better accommodations soon. We can't keep doing this for long."

He looked at her steadily. "We're used to it."

"I'm not. I demand a bed, a real one."

There was a ghost of a smile, and the corner of his lips twitched. "Duly noted."

She turned to Damon and asked, "Are you driving?"

"Yes, I am."

And, with that, they headed out to the truck.

THEY EXITED, LEAVING Terk locked in the warehouse.

"Even if we had another warehouse," Tasha muttered to herself, "we could at least put beds in there."

"We're not sure if we can get a second one," he murmured, "but we do have a better bed coming now than just that mat on the floor." He started up the truck, then waited until she was buckled in to back out of the lot. "Do you know where you want to go?"

"Yes." She named two storefronts.

"Good enough, as long as you know how to get there."

"Well, GPS does," she quipped, "and he happens to be my friend."

At that, he laughed and followed directions, getting to the first storefront within about fifteen minutes.

"Let's hope they still have fresh bread," she muttered.

"Hey, it's not that late."

"It's late enough for Paris." She hopped out and walked into the store, while he sat and watched.

They hadn't been followed, and, as far as he could tell, nobody was tracking them. But it would be pretty obvious if they kept any truck parked at the open car park. A multilevel vehicle lot was on the other side. He was thinking about doing long-term parking there and moving it around, switching up vehicles too. Anything that was a routine more than three days was too much.

They didn't want to attract attention, and, while vehicles permanently parked at the warehouses weren't unusual, because there were lots of others, new ones would be. Coming and going periodically may or may not attract attention; he wasn't sure. It currently was the best they could do on a short-term basis, but something better for the long haul would have to happen soon.

He knew that Levi was tracking down something that was workable for them long-term. Terk was by far more sensitive to energies on electricity than Damon was. He could work from anywhere, but then he didn't have the range that Terk did. And Damon hadn't really put his abilities to any kind of use yet. Mostly because of the pain involved, since he knew that he only had half of his normal capability, if that.

Half. He'd never been half anything in his life, but now he was at half power, half use, and it made him feel like he was useless and a failure. But he had to shake off that feeling and do what he could do. When he thought about it rationally, he knew that even with only half, or none of those special abilities, he was a better and more capable man than most.

He watched as she came out of the store, carrying two bags, one stuffed with several loaves of bread. She hopped into the truck with a big fat smile on her face, as the aroma of fresh-baked bread filled the cab.

"God, that smells good," he muttered. He turned on the engine, quickly backed out of the parking lot, and asked, "Now where?"

Then she directed him to the second location. Once again, he sat inside while she dove into the storefront, only to return ten to fifteen minutes later with another two bags.

He looked at the food, shook his head. "You do know that you have enough food here for a dozen people."

"Or three of us who are hungry and can make three meals of this," she declared. "Now we can go home again."

She even said *home* in a natural tone of voice. He wondered at that but kept on going and drove back to the warehouse lot. He dropped her off and explained, "I'll park across the street."

Then he pulled the truck back around and buried it in the multilevel parking lot just down the way. He walked back, then loped across the more or less empty parking lot of the warehouse units. The entrance to theirs was slightly out of the way, and that was a good thing. Even now, he wandered about, as if he were looking to purchase a storage locker or rent one. He checked the place out, looking to see what was different from the last couple days. Honestly it looked all the same, as if the vehicles were in long-term parking too.

Finally letting himself back inside again, he heard Terk and Tasha chattering cheerfully. Tasha was happily slicing a baguette into big, long angled slices and buttering them, while Terk was slicing up different cheeses and meats.

Damon's stomach immediately growled.

She looked over at him, smiled. "Oh, so you are hungry after all. Aren't you the one who thought I got enough for a dozen people? Listening to your stomach complain, I'm not certain we'll have enough for you."

He grinned, loving the fact that they were back to a more effortless and friendly tone, although she had rarely teased him as she did with the rest of the team. As he looked down at all the sliced finger foods, he reached over and grabbed something. When he took a look at the bigger selection of meat and cheeses, the smaller groupings of more perishable fruits, he realized she'd provided a small feast. He quickly loaded up with ham and a couple different cheeses on his two slices of bread and sat down on the nearby chair and munched away. "Nothing quite like fresh bread."

Then she opened a bag and brought out still-warm croissants.

His eyebrows shot up. "I didn't realize you got those too."

And she pointed at a couple round loaves as well.

"I guess we're good for the day then." He chuckled.

"We are." She gently broke apart a tender croissant, flakes of buttery pastry falling onto the bag she had pulled it from. "And it's warm," she crowed in delight. She had two.

While Damon watched, he realized there would be a shortage soon if he didn't grab his own, so he snatched up two himself. "Terk, you better get some, before she eats it all."

They all shared a laugh and bantered a bit as they ate. By the time they finished, and Damon sat here with a cup of coffee, he felt some of the stress and tension inside him waning.

"We haven't done too badly for the first twenty-four hours." Damon looked over at Terk. A shadow crossed his face. "Unless you have any news to add?"

"No, we've done not bad," Terk admitted. "We have communications up and running. We have another security company attached and helping. We're doing searches on prior adversaries and other potential threats. We have our own team members all under lock and guard." He nodded. "And we're here, with the three of us at least functioning, more or less."

"I wish Mera were here." Tasha sighed. "It would make my job easier."

"I didn't get the impression she would be ready for that for a while," Terk murmured.

Tasha shook her head. "I know. And, when I think of the fact that Wilson will never be ready, I can't really complain, can I?"

"It's the nature of the human being," he noted. "We complain, even though we know better and can't change it."

"Why is that?"

"I think because we want something different than what we've got. And it doesn't matter because we will remember Wilson for the crazy cheerful and incredibly efficient person he was." Terk paused. "And hope to God his family remembers him with a smile," he murmured.

"I hope so. Letting them know would be terrible. He didn't deserve this," she muttered. "Neither did Mera."

"Neither did the rest of the team," Damon reminded her. "But this is where we're at."

"And where exactly is that?" she asked. "Now that we're set up, who are we trying to locate first?"

"My vote is whoever killed Wilson," Terk said instantly. "And he will lead us to the next step."

She stared at him in surprise. "Okay, I guess I wasn't thinking of that."

"Well, you weren't *not* thinking of it," Damon added, "since you were already checking to see where and what there were for vehicles and faces around his place."

"No, I guess you're right," she agreed. "I just wasn't necessarily thinking of that as a focus. But then, honestly, I've been pretty scattered. This whole thing has got me rattled."

"Of course it has," Terk murmured. "And you're surely not the only one. We're in this together. Remember that."

She nodded and smiled at him. "Got it."

Damon watched the interplay, wondering how Terk always managed to make her feel so comfortable and at home, while she was stiff with Damon. Then again, Terk was a friend, while Damon had deliberately kept himself out of that category.

How foolish of him.

CHAPTER 9

THE DAY PASSED in a flurry of tracking information. Tasha settled into her routine, one that she'd thought she would never get back to. When she had found out that the government would be closing them down within days, she'd been heartbroken and yet almost euphoric because it meant a change in her life, one that she was ready for. This scenario was far from the change she'd expected though. It felt like the same thing to a degree but without the official compass, without the umbrella of protection, without the full team. Nor did they have the same resources. Although, as she was finding out, they had plenty of money. "How come we have money?"

"Because we still have access to the bank account. We always did, since it was set up under my name," Terk said.

She looked at him sharply. "And they didn't change that?"

He smiled. "I never gave them access. I didn't want them digging in and removing money when we needed it."

She burst out laughing. "Oh my, that's perfect." Then she frowned. "But that also means, if you use any money, they'll know that you're alive and well."

He nodded. "Which is why I changed the name to something else."

"Interesting," she murmured quietly. "What did you

choose?"

"A mock name. One that nobody knows and one that doesn't lead anywhere."

"So then you think we're safe?"

"We're safe. We have access to the money, and we'll pull it as we need it."

"Good enough because I highly doubt you have much for weapons, do you?"

"We have some, as you've seen, but we'll get more."

"And yet we can't use the same supplier."

"We can, but we'll need a middleman."

"Great, and who will that be?"

"Merk is on his way over."

"No way," she said. "He's your brother. Surely he'll look like you to some degree."

He stopped, shook his head. "He'll be in disguise."

She withheld a comment on that because Terk had very strong features. She highly doubted that Merk would look anything less. But she'd been wrong before, so who knew? "If you say so," she muttered.

He chuckled. "Have a little faith."

"I kind of lost that a while back."

"I know. I see that, but don't be so lost that we can't pull you back."

"I don't even know what that means," she muttered.

"Anything else on the tracking?"

"No." She shook her head. "I did track down little bits on the vehicles seen around Wilson's and Mera's places. But I never did get sight of them on the cameras around mine and lost them a few blocks away in car parks."

"What does the time stamp show for each of the three hits?"

Tasha knew he would ask that. "Wilson first, Mera second, me last, with a quick in-and-out assassination and the allotted travel time in between."

"As expected. Still doesn't mean the same person was the killer for each, doesn't mean that they drove the same truck, doesn't mean that they drove a truck at all," he reminded her.

"I know. I know," she said. "I was looking for something definitive that would tie to the three of us."

"*Definitive* won't be part of our world for a while."

"That's not fair," she complained. "How will we know if we got the bad guys or who the bad guys even are if we don't have proof?"

"We'll get the proof." Terk's tone brooked no disagreement. "No argument on that. But it's likely to be a slightly different process than we've seen before."

She wasn't even sure what to say to that and didn't like the sound of it at all. But she also knew that, right now, their lives were in danger—all of them, the three here, but what about the other team members and ... "Do you think Mera is okay?"

"She is right now. She's moved to another location," Terk shared.

She looked at him. "You didn't tell me."

"Nope, I didn't."

"Is that a trust issue?"

"No, not at all," he stated. "It's just a simple matter of, if you were caught, you can't tell anybody what you don't know."

"Right," she said, not exactly wanting to hear talk of getting *caught*. "I keep forgetting that level of need-to-know and why. I guess I wanted to think that we were a whole lot closer as a family unit now."

"It's not about that," he explained. "But, if you are taken down, we can't have you holding information that'll hurt the rest of us."

"You know that I'd never give it up, right?"

"When they've broken both your arms, broken every toe in your body, split open your leg, and used other nasty elements of torture," he explained in gruesome detail, "you'll tell them anything to make it stop. Don't ever misjudge the level of torture that these people would do. They kill without a thought, and they will do so again."

She stared at him, knowing that the color on her face had probably bleached out. "I forgot you're always so brutally honest."

"Brutally honest," he stated, "that's what counts."

She nodded. "I got it." She swallowed. "So do we know who else is coming with Merk?"

"Maybe nobody." Terk shrugged. "I'm not sure."

"Will we have any contact with them?"

"Not directly, no. We can't risk it."

She frowned at that. She'd known the likely answer before she had even asked and even understood it, but she still didn't like it. Not at all. "We're really isolated now, aren't we?"

"We are," he said cheerfully. "And believe me. That's a good way to be."

"I don't understand."

"We don't have to worry about other people stabbing us in the back anymore," he admitted. "It's just us. We only have to trust each other, and, therefore, we're safe."

She nodded. "I guess, but it still seems odd."

"It's odd because it's not what we're used to, but that

doesn't mean it's wrong."

"I get that too." For the next bit she was quiet, as she thought it over. "There's got to be something else we can do though."

"We're doing quite a bit," Terk acknowledged. "Make sure you have monitoring going on around us here," he suggested. "No way to know for sure if we've been followed on any of these outside trips."

"I do have it set up," she noted. "I hope you are getting in more security cams?"

"We have a lot of equipment coming in today, and some of it is coming with Merk."

"So, there'll be a drop shipment or something?"

"Yep, and it should be coming any minute." Just then his phone beeped with a text notification. "And there it is." He smiled, with a note of satisfaction. "I do like it when people are dependable."

"And where is it?" she asked, hopping to her feet.

He smiled, walked over to another door that she had basically ignored because a bunch of junk was piled up in front of it.

He moved aside all the junk, with an assist from Damon, who had immediately hopped up to help. As soon as the door was unlocked, she followed them into the next room, where Terk flicked on lights to reveal the room was full of boxes.

"What is this?" she asked. And then she spied several beds off to the side. "Oh." She stopped, and then she grinned. "I did demand a bed, didn't I?"

"You did," he agreed, "and I take demands like that very serious."

She burst out laughing. "So will this be our hidey-hole

then?" She turned, looked at him. "I'm not sure it'll be good for you though."

"It's what I've got." Terk shrugged. "So it doesn't matter if it's good or not. I'll work with it."

She frowned. "But I know that you need more in terms of protection."

"I do," he agreed, "and I'm working on building up something in here. Honestly I find the concrete is almost soothing. More storage is above and on the other side as well. So we are surrounded by a lot of concrete. Not as good as steel but it's something."

"But you need steel to stop people from tracking you, don't you?"

"Yes," he noted quietly, "so we'll use the fact that people can track us to our advantage."

She sucked in her breath when she understood. "You're trying to set a trap?"

He gave her a ghost of a smile. "I'd do any damn thing I could to make this work," he stated. "So a trap? Yes."

"And me?"

"You'll be on the other side of this building," he promised, "and hopefully not even nearby before that trap is sprung."

"But you can't know that," she muttered, glaring at him.

"Nope, I can't," he admitted, "and that's part and parcel of what this is all about. We have to make sure that we're protected and must do whatever we can to ensure, if they come after us, that we've got them. I don't want any more surprises, like ambushes."

"No." She sighed in frustration. "I get that."

"Good." Terk nodded. "Then you'll understand perfectly when I tell you that you'll be in here more often than not."

She glared at him. "Are we moving the computer equipment in then?"

"Maybe." He studied the area. "Or maybe it would be better to separate the working space from the sleeping space."

"That would be good," she agreed. "It'll be rough having all of us here together."

"Not that rough," he stated. "Damon and I have worked together for a long time, so I don't think it'll be all that difficult at all."

"It's just me who'll have to get used to roughing it, is that it?"

He laughed. "You're young. You're adaptable. So you can get used to anything you want. After all, it's really just a mind-set."

AFTER ANOTHER TEXT message, Terk held up his phone. "Merk is being followed."

It was startling, but Terk's exclamation disturbed the silence, as Damon and Tasha worked. They both turned and stared at him. "Shit, does he know who it is?"

"Black truck." Terk's tone was clipped, obviously his patience at a premium. "So likely the same guy who killed Wilson."

"And that's a huge break," Damon put in, walking closer to Terk. "Where is he?"

"Leading him away from us and looking for a place to set up a trap." Looking at Damon, Terk asked, "You want in on a sting?"

"Sure as hell do," he snapped. "Tell me where and

when."

"That's what Merk is looking for. He wants to keep him away from here but doesn't want to take a chance of losing this lead."

Tasha hopped up and walked over. "I'm in."

Immediately both men frowned at her, but she shook her head. "None of that," she scolded. "We don't have any other people here. It's just the three of us, so, if any of this goes down wrong, we still need somebody left standing who can set up a new team and a new sting to get these assholes," she stated in a determined voice.

The two men exchanged glances, and Damon didn't know what to think. She had elementary training, as all agents did, but it's not like she was trained the way the rest of them were. "I don't like it," he said bluntly.

"I know you don't like it," she replied, with a sugar-sweet smile. "But we're not here to talk about you."

He burst out laughing at that. "Good point."

"You realize you may not come back?" she asked.

"Bigger than that," Terk snapped, "is the fact that Damon's attention will be split because he'll also be looking after you."

She glared at Terk, and Damon had to appreciate the fact that she had the balls to stand up to him. But Terk had a point. "I know you don't like to think about it," Damon told her, "but he's right. I will be splitting my energy, trying to make sure that you're safe, so I won't focus 100 percent on getting this guy."

"But you'll have Merk, right?"

He frowned and nodded. "Yes."

"So let me run a vehicle. Let me do something," she suggested. "I need to be involved somehow."

"Well, we need a command center, and we've always needed that," Damon stated. "I don't know that you appreciate how important that job is."

She groaned. "But that's what I always do."

His grin was immediately infectious. "And that's because you're damn good at it. If anybody can handle the electronics, it's you," he stated, "and we need you here for that."

She glared, but he could tell from the soft slump of her shoulders that she could see the sense in that.

With relief he turned to Terk. "I want you to stay here too."

"Oh, hell no," Terk snapped. "Don't give me that shit."

"I'm only running with half senses," Damon said. "You're the only one who's got your senses left and alive to function with. You find a way to get my damn senses back, and it'll be different then. She's right. There's got to be one of us standing at the end. One of the two of us has to be left, and, since you're protecting the team, you are it. And it's got to be me as part of this sting."

The two men glared at each other, but it was hard to argue with the common sense Damon had put forth. Nobody liked what was happening, but, until they got more team members back, this is just where it was at.

"You know I'm right," Damon stated. "As much as I don't like it, it's what we have to work with." He was already collecting the stuff he needed, and, as he walked over to the table, he snatched the truck keys, shot a look at both of them, and ordered, "Stay here." And, with that, he returned his attention to getting ready.

She glared at Terk. "You can't always protect me," she murmured.

His lips twisted into a half rueful and half tender smile.

"We almost lost so many," he replied quietly. "You need to allow yourself to be protected."

She fisted her hands on her hips and glared back. "I lost them too." Tears choked the back of her throat. "You need to let me help."

"Agreed." Terk nodded. "So please do what you can—from here. Doing what you do. Tracking. We've got trackers on the truck. We've got trackers on Merk. Please follow them. Give me the satellite feed and let me know if anything's there. At least then I can tell Merk if he's walking into a problem."

Her eyebrows shot up. "Is that because of your normal senses or because you're twins?"

"Both," he noted. "Twins always have a special relationship, and my abilities just made it that much easier."

"How is it that you have these special skills and he doesn't?" she muttered.

Damon heard the bulk of their conversation as he geared up; then he bolted out to the truck. He left them to their discussion, and, as much as he wanted to be part of it, he needed to head out and to see if they could catch this asshole who was trailing Merk. As soon as Damon was out of the parking lot, he contacted Terk on his phone, propped it up on the dashboard, and asked, "So did you come up with the location?"

"I did. Sending you the address right now."

As soon as he punched it in, he looked at the GPS map as he drove toward it. "It looks pretty protected," he noted cautiously.

"It is, but it's also deserted right now. The company is off on a trip for team building or some such thing," he noted, disgust in his voice.

Damon barely held back his own grin. "You know that a lot of corporate places do that."

"Right, so they shut down the entire company for it," Terk snorted. "How on earth is that productive?"

"Who knows? Maybe they all needed a break?"

"Well, the corporate buildings are empty. The parking lot is empty, and a few company vehicles are parked in the lot, so you should find lots of space there."

"A little hard to hide though."

"Not so much," he noted. "They have a vertical parking area you could get in, and they'll have to go hunting to see where you are."

"Got it," he replied. "Where's Merk?"

"On the second level already."

"In hiding?"

"Waiting," Terk clarified. "I've got him on the other phone, and, so far, he's not seeing anything."

"No, he won't see it. You know they'll come in without any warning. And you know as well as I do that, although they sent a hired assassin to take out Wilson and Mera, they used something much more powerful to take out our team. So Merk could be getting either of those coming at him."

"I don't think they'll expect him to have any skills, but we've already considered that fact."

"Can you protect him?"

"I'll do my damnedest," Terk said. "My brother has always been special in many ways. But he's never really been able to handle this energy work."

"No, but he has accepted it and you, and that's worth everything."

"It always is," Terk replied quietly. "But we've never really discussed it in any detail, so I don't think he understands what we do exactly."

At that, Damon snorted. "Who the hell does? Sometimes I don't understand it myself."

A ghost of a smile was in Terk's voice when he laughed. "True enough, and we've been getting stronger all the time."

"Do you suppose that's why they took us out?" he murmured. "Were they afraid of us? Of what we could do? If they could control us?"

"I think it's a good possibility."

"How did they know?"

"I don't know." Terk paused. "I hate to say it, but it keeps crossing my mind that we potentially had somebody leaking information."

"Are you saying we had a mole?"

"I think that's a strong word to use because I'm not sure this person knew they were being used."

"That makes it even harder. Surely you don't suspect Tasha?"

"No, I don't, and she's pretty bloody angry at whoever did this to all of us."

"But then she would be, if she thought she had been used to hurt those she cares about."

"It could also have been done under the guise of it being part of their job. So they wouldn't realize they had done anything wrong."

"It sure as hell better not be any of us," Damon muttered, "but I can see that they might have tried that."

"The other possibility is that we were bugged."

"Did we ever really have those kinds of discussions in the office?"

"No, not really," Terk said thoughtfully. "But I'm at a loss to explain how else."

"Was anything else bugged?" he asked. "Like, I know it sounds foolish, but we've got trackers on us now. Did we have anything on us back then that might have given them audio?"

"I would hope not," Terk replied, his voice turning distant. "And I'm not getting any sense of that."

"Well, keep it in your thought process as we head into this mess right now because we'll need to know just where that leak came from. And I don't know if there's any way for her to tell, but you might want to ask Tasha to look into it."

"I will. You take care of yourself."

"Oh, don't worry," he said. "I'm already in the car park. Several vehicles are here, so I'm wondering if they all got picked up on a charter bus or something."

"That's exactly what they did. That's another reason why it's a good place to park because nobody knows what's going on."

"Good enough. I'm pulling into the bottom level."

"And where will you go?"

"I'll just park down here," he decided calmly, "and then I can disappear."

"Okay, I'll tell Merk. Watch your back." With that, Terk hung up.

Damon parked in between two cars, leaving himself plenty of room to get in and out as needed. He slipped out, closed the truck door quietly, then, moving around the other vehicles, came up to the stairs. He quickly shifted downstairs, looking to see what was there, but it looked like a ground-level access area only. Frowning at that because it was not really accessible by car, it was still a hell of a place for people to sneak in, if they wanted to.

He saw stairs and an elevator. "I wonder if you have access to the main buildings from here," he muttered. He wouldn't be at all surprised. And from the building perspective, it gave access for everybody in the main buildings. He walked over in the dark because these were just concrete car parks. Didn't appear to be any lighting, until darkness settled in, and then emergency lighting would shine. The door itself was locked; he checked it and realized he could easily unlock it, but that's not where he was going right now.

Sliding back through the shadows, he headed to the stairwell and just then heard a tap above him. He froze, and then the tap came again, twice. He responded with a code that he and Terk knew, but Damon wasn't expecting anybody else to know. When it was answered, he realized that Merk had an awful lot more in common with Terk than Damon had expected.

And before Damon realized it, a quiet voice was at his shoulder.

"How is my brother?"

Damon didn't turn, but he whispered, "He's fine but dealing with a lot of trauma right now."

"I'm surprised to see you here," the man said, a hint of suspicion in his voice.

Damon stiffened at that, turned, and faced a man who looked so much like Terk that it shocked him. He studied the face in front of him, seeing the change in the glint of the eyes, a slightly heftier build of someone who worked out harder and heavier than Terk did, but with the same strong jaw, the same cut cheekbones, and that gaze that pierced him in place. "You must be Merk."

"What gave that away?" he drawled.

Damon flashed a grin. "Any sign of him?"

"In the parking lot."

"The parkade?"

Merk shook his head. "On the ground lot."

"Did he exit the truck?"

"No, hasn't left yet."

"What do you think he's waiting for?"

"My guess would be you," he said in that same slow tone.

"Damn." Damon shook his head. "Looking at you, it's kind of scary."

"Twins are like that," he noted, "but there's just enough differences that you shouldn't make a mistake between us," he stated, almost a note of warning.

"That won't happen," Damon declared. "Terk has some mad skills. I don't know what you've got."

"Mad skills in a very different way," he stated calmly. "My brother has always been the one with the otherworldly skills. But don't get ahead of yourself. I'll take you out in two seconds flat if I don't like what you're doing."

Damon stared at him and recognized a warrior within the same space he was in. "I'm not your problem, but someone took out our team, and those are the assholes I want. Just so we understand each other," he stated.

Merk's body untensed.

Damon realized that he had passed whatever test Merk needed in order for Damon to be of assistance. "Did you see or get any visual on whoever is driving?"

"No," he replied, "except for a baseball cap."

"The notorious baseball cap," Damon muttered. "What a pain in the ass those things are."

"Very effective. We've sure used them more than a few times ourselves."

"Exactly," Damon agreed, "but I don't know what kind

of attack we're looking for."

"Anything that works."

"You realize that it's quite possible it could be a psychic energy attack, like that which took out the rest of our team, and that you could potentially be affected by it."

"Not as much as you. I don't have energy abilities to get blocked," he noted calmly. "It's one of the reasons I'm here now."

"And you're okay not to see Terk?"

"He'd be pissed if I tried to see him," Merk admitted. "He wants to know that I'm safe."

"Has he always been that way?"

"Always," he stated. "He went his own way because he had his own path to walk, and I couldn't help him with it, and sometimes that was damn hard. But he has always been a protector and always been somebody who tried to keep his personal life out of it."

"Somehow I doubt that you're any different."

"Nope, I'm sure not," he said, "but now both he and I have higher stakes. I have a partner, and he apparently has a child on the way."

Just enough anger was mixed with a note of humor for Damon to realize that Merk was as shocked by that turn of events as Terk was. "Who the hell knew something like this would happen?" Damon muttered.

"It's one thing to not know it would happen, but who had any idea that somebody would even think of doing something like this?"

"Whenever you end up with assholes," Damon murmured, "you end up with assholes willing to do whatever it takes."

Just then, with his senses open as wide as they could be

because they were only operating halfway, he sent out a probe through the parking lot, looking for any signs of life. As he did so, he sensed somebody staring. "Definitely somebody out there."

"Yep, there is," Merk agreed. "I watched the vehicle drive in."

"So he didn't see you come in here?"

"I think he probably did, and he's also waiting for me to come out."

"*Hmm*, that also means he saw me come in."

"Yep." And Merk didn't say anything more about that.

Just a noncommittal *yep*, and Damon had to love it. This was somebody who understood both the good and the bad of the way it had played out. That they could have a problem, or it could be a solution. "He's probably looking for both of us, just to see what or who it is that you're meeting."

"I would expect so, but if they didn't have any tracker on your truck, they've got it now."

"I won't take it back again," Damon replied carelessly. "That was always part of the plan."

"Good, I'd still like to make sure that we take this guy though."

"Agreed. We need answers, but we'll need somebody alive to get them."

"You think he'll let himself get taken?" Merk asked, with a note of amusement.

"Well, I wouldn't, would you?"

"Hell no. But, on the other hand, I'd never expect to get taken in the first place." And, with that, he moved out.

Damon was surprised, yet not surprised. He didn't even know how to explain how he felt about seeing this replica of

Terk. Just as hard, just as obviously capable, and just as confident as the man he knew so well. And to think that it was a brother, somebody different and yet the same. It wasn't shocking, but Damon couldn't quite come up with the word for what it was.

Maybe it was because his senses were down or because of the fatigue that always sat at the back of his mind. Maybe it was the sudden turn of events, but Damon knew without a single doubt that he could trust this man as much as he trusted Terk. And, with that thought prominent, he followed Merk as they headed to the bottom level and then outside to where the ground parking lot was. "You got a game plan?" Damon asked, as he caught up.

"Hell yeah," Merk replied. "I'll open that truck and haul out this asshole and ask him some questions."

CHAPTER 10

I T WAS HARD to listen to Terk's reasoning and to not see the logic of it herself, but Tasha still didn't like it. She didn't like anything about it. And then she realized that the feelings for Damon she had tried so hard to squash down were there regardless. She sat down at her computer, a cup of coffee in hand, as she watched the interaction on screen. "Both men are on the move."

"Yeah, I can feel them." Terk got up and came to stand beside her. "They're heading into the open parking lot itself, which is all the more interesting."

She tapped the screen where a black truck stuck in between two other trucks on the parking lot. "That's him. What do you think they'll do?"

"Knowing my brother, he'll probably walk right up there and pull the asshole from the cab."

She gasped, stared at him. "Won't that get him killed?"

"Depends on whether the guy is expecting it or not. Merk is pretty wild, and he's got some pretty fast moves. But he's also a straight-up guy, who tends to deal with problems head-on."

"Interesting. You guys must have had fun growing up."

"We fought plenty, if that's what you're getting at," he admitted. "Both of us are very dominant, and, once I realized what was going on in my headspace and that he didn't match it, there was an even bigger separation. But, once Merk realized that, in a way, it made me weaker, he immediately stepped up as a protector," he murmured. "Not a whole lot we wouldn't do for each other."

"Have you ever saved his life?"

He laughed. "A couple times. Mostly when I get a heads-up that something was going on in their world. I would just send them a notice and let them know things are wonky. If nothing else, I figure it will make them a little bit more respectful of what they've got going, knowing something's out there that they need to be a little more prepared for."

"Sounds like a fascinating life."

"It is, and it isn't," he replied quietly. "Definitely a lot of good things about having insight when things go wrong, but, when things go wrong, and you didn't see it or interpret it correctly, believe me, an awful lot of recrimination and guilt result."

"Because you didn't see what happened, did you?"

"No, I didn't. If you're talking about Wilson, I didn't see that at all. I didn't see the team getting blown up either, even though a part of me wondered," he noted. "I had been given enough assurances from the higher-ups that I thought we would be safe. Obviously I was wrong, and believe me, nobody feels that guilt more than I do," he murmured. "It's a shitty deal all the way around."

"The thing is," she noted, "you can only do so much. Humanity still has to step up and to accept responsibility for the shit they do themselves. You couldn't have known for sure what would happen. You didn't get any warning, not even an inkling, and that says a lot in itself."

"Exactly. It says that these people who took down the team put some block out ahead of them coming, and that worries me even more."

"You really want to take them out, don't you?"

"I do," he murmured quietly. "They're a threat to us all."

"And a threat we can't see, which is even more worrisome," she said. "But then isn't that what they would say about you?"

"I think it's what they've already said, and it's likely how they justified what they did," he murmured. "The trouble is, I'm just not sure who hired them. That makes me even more concerned."

"Because you think it was our government?"

"No, not at all," he argued, "but I do think that it was a government—or at least a faction within a government—looking to protect their own. And I get that. I really do. But, at the same time, they brought it to us, when it didn't need to happen. We weren't in a fight. We weren't in a war. Nothing was going on that they had to deal with. So this was a purely offensive strike. It was preemptive, and that, to me, is unacceptable."

"Interesting," she noted, "because I feel like we have heard that from you before."

"Maybe, maybe not," he replied. "Nothing like being attacked in the dark to cause a shift of your own mind-set."

"And yet would you ever change what you do?"

"Only how I do it," he answered in a somewhat cryptic tone, and, with that, he walked back to his corner.

She watched as he immediately closed his eyes, and, almost like a plug was pulled, his body shifted. She'd seen him go in and out before. And he was still doing it but almost like a steadier process now. She didn't know whether it was a lack of trust or if it was the fact that he didn't have the space and the privacy he needed to do what he did. She worried about that because she didn't want him feeling like he couldn't trust her; yet, at the same time, she had no place to go, and he had deliberately not gone into the other room. So he felt like he had no place he could go either, which had to be hard.

Without any answers to give him, she watched her screen as the men approached the truck. "I don't know if you can tell what's going on, but, outside of seeing two moving toward the truck," she relayed, "I'm not seeing anything."

Just then her burner phone of the day buzzed. She picked it up. "Damon, what's up?"

"The truck is empty. Did you see anything?"

"No, I didn't," she replied. "Where could he have gone?"

"Oh, he's here," he stated, "but somehow he managed to get out of the truck, and we didn't notice."

"Is there a side door he could have opened and shut?"

"Possibly. Obviously he's gone, but he's not very far away."

"Or he set some sort of trap, so be damn careful."

"We're on it. Did Terk get anything?"

"Nothing specific yet," Terk answered, "except he's there."

"Yeah, he's here all right. We just don't know where." And, with that, Damon hung up.

Without even looking at Terk, she confirmed, "The guy isn't in the truck."

"They're looking for answers. He needs to check again," Terk said in an odd voice.

Frowning, she wondered about that but snatched up her phone and quickly sent Damon a text, giving them Terk's message. She knew it wouldn't make much sense. She could see the location of the trackers on her screen, but she couldn't necessarily see exactly what was going on, and that was frustrating. She leaned forward and tried to watch, and then what even made her feel worse was a sudden jerk in her camera feed. She gasped.

"It's okay," Terk stated, "neither were hit."

"Neither were hit, but they're being fired at," she snapped.

"They are, indeed," he murmured, his eyes closed. "I'll see what I can do."

She turned and looked at him, not sure what he even meant by that. She'd always been fascinated to know that some supernatural element was involved with what they were doing, but she never really understood what it was. He'd always just explained it was cold-war training and that sometimes it worked and sometimes it didn't. And, honest to God, most times she thought it didn't work, compared to good old-fashioned fieldwork.

But she didn't know for sure what worked and what didn't. Nobody ever talked about it. None of the admins even gave voice to all the questions in their heads, except Wilson. He had asked her a couple times just what these guys could really do, but she hadn't been able to answer him. They had mused privately over it all, but nobody had come up with any direct techniques that could have been utilized. It fascinated her but, at the same time, had also frustrated her to no end.

Now, for the first time, she wondered if Wilson had a reason for the questions. She tried to remember everything that had been asked, but it was hard because Mera had had questions too. On that note Tasha contacted Mera, sending a text. **Hey, do you remember ever being asked odd**

questions about the team? Like, what we did, what we didn't do, or anything that would trigger some suspicion on your part? Obviously I'm still pondering what the hell is going on with this mess.

When she didn't get an answer, she frowned. Of course there was no reason for Mera to answer, but there was also no reason for her not to, unless she really was serious about having nothing to do with them anymore. Tasha sent a question mark and then asked if Mera were okay.

When Tasha still got no answer, she really started to get worried. Mera had been doing the same kind of work for three years with them now. But, as Tasha stared at the shadow on the screen that was Damon, she realized that, for the first time, her heart really was involved, and the stakes were higher than ever before. She could only hope that whatever the hell was going on in that strange online pantomime she was watching was something Damon and Merk could handle.

She didn't think she could deal with much more of this bullshit.

AS THEY APPROACHED the truck for the second time, Damon checked under the tarp. They'd already looked once, but they hadn't realized that the tarp half hid a box in the front. He hopped up into the truck bed, not caring if they were seen or not. He pulled the tarp free, walked over to the box, and noted it was locked. He kicked it hard with his boot, shattering the hinge on it, and, as soon as he lifted the lid, he knew. With a hard expression on his face, he looked over at Merk. "Is this the guy?"

Merk hopped up beside him, swore, then pulled out his phone and nodded. "Yeah, that's him." He took a picture and sent it off immediately, presumably to Ice.

Damon looked back at Merk. "We need to get out of here."

"Yeah, we do."

They jumped over either side and immediately ran out of the parking lot. Damon went left; Merk went right. They were trying to split up, and, if any tails were nearby or if any cameras were watching them, they needed to find a way to disappear—and fast. They had left their two vehicles inside the car park, but any other vehicles left there now would be very suspect.

Damon kept going left, following any exiting vehicles, then running through the bush, trying to find a place to get out of the potential camera zone. With satellites and drones these days, just no way to know, so you always had to assume that you were being tracked.

And he *was* being tracked, of course; he had his own tracker. And, with that thought, he winced. He pulled out his phone and called Tasha. "Can you see me?"

"Yes."

"Can you tell if anybody else is tracking me?"

He heard her suck back her breath. "No, that's not something that I can tell."

"Can you shut down my tracker?"

"I can, but I won't," she stated in a hard voice. "That's the only way we have to know that you're safe."

"I don't give a fuck," he snapped. "Shut it down, or I'm ripping it out. Do it now."

"Terk?" she asked, wanting a second opinion.

"He has been tracked, so knock it down."

Damon heard her cursing in the background, and he called out through the phone, "Thanks. Terk. If you got anything to give me a hand, I could sure use it."

"On it," Terk said.

Damon stepped through a hedge to the other side, then looked around and felt an odd sensation coming down over him. He stopped, closed his eyes, and recognized Terk's signature. He sent back a message to Terk, hoping that he would receive it. Damon wasn't the best at this stuff, but he could communicate. *I'm safe. Keep her safe. I'll call when I can.* Then Damon sent one last message. *See if you can track this energy.* And, with that, he shut things down.

Then he shifted into what looked like a series of office buildings. He moved silently through them, keeping his awareness at half-mast, knowing that a mistake at this point in time would be critical. It was good to be a transmitter, but, if you didn't have anybody who could receive, it was no good. But he was a receiver *and* a transmitter, though at half power, it didn't seem to matter. He would suffer no matter what.

He stayed on the move, slipping from vehicle to vehicle, store to store, office building to office building, weaving through and back, in and out of exits, as he skirted his way around a huge ten-block radius from where he'd left his vehicle. By the time he made it into the car park again, six hours had lapsed. He knew he hadn't been seen coming in because he had actually broken into an office and gone through the underground tunnel made of thick concrete.

As he sat here in his truck, he sent a message to Terk. *At vehicle. Looked for obvious tracker. Found none. How about you?*

When nothing came back, he fired up the engine, slowly

backed out, and hit the road, then turned and headed back home again. Damon saw no apparent sign of anybody following him. But that didn't mean they didn't have somebody at a distance who could lock on his location via satellite or drone or energy work or whatever and see what Damon was doing. That was always the part that got him.

Terk was good at that; he could lock on somebody forty miles away, actually see him just sitting in a room some-where, building a bomb or whatever. They had had success with Terk tracking down that same person, when he went out in a vehicle again. That's the part that got Damon right now because, if stuff like that was happening, where the bad guys could follow Terk's team's energy signatures …

He beefed up the shield around him a little bit more, burning through a ton of his energy, which was in low supply and was why he hadn't been doing that before. He'd been moving fast enough for the last six hours that even Terk couldn't keep his energy on Damon. But now that he was driving and heading back to their temporary headquarters again, he needed to make sure he was shielded. He had to protect Tasha and Terk from being found. But what was Damon to do when his energy was down to less than 10 percent?

Damon had been running hard and fast, so he was out of energy, out of food, and pretty quickly out of any kind of resources. When he got back to where their warehouse was, he parked down in the shopping mall around the corner, then took a circuitous way around and moved in with a large group going into a nearby storage unit to unload furniture. With that, he slipped into the second building and then walked around to the respective doorway, where he got in all on his own.

He stepped inside, and all he heard was dead silence. His heart slammed against his chest because he knew it already.

No one was here.

CHAPTER 11

"I DON'T WANT to leave him," Tasha balked.

"Don't argue with me," Terk said. "We're leaving now."

She glared at him, but he motioned for her to exit the warehouse. She pointed at the secret room. "That's why we have the second room."

"I know," he agreed, "but somebody is sending out probes."

At that, she stopped, startled. "Seriously?"

He nodded. "A lot of our energy reveals we are here, plus a lot of our digital products can be verified as here, and everything has been touched by us, so you can bet that this is a big energy hub. I've got a blockade up, but I can't shield all of us."

"So what do you want to do?"

"We'll go in a very public place, where they can't separate us from the others."

"So, the mall across the way?"

He thought about it and then nodded. "Yeah. We have to do some shopping anyway."

She watched as he led the way, his hand on hers the whole time. "Is there a reason we're holding hands?"

He nodded, and, speaking in a low voice from the side of his mouth, he whispered, "Pretend to be happy."

She snorted. "I'm thrilled."

"You don't have to go overboard," he noted. "But, as long as you're attached to me, then I can shield you. But, if I can't shield you, then anybody searching for us, especially from a distance, can lock on to me and, therefore, find you."

Instantly she stepped closer to him.

"Thanks, that makes it easier."

"It's all you had to say," she snapped. "For crying out loud, we can walk with our arms around each other for all I care."

He grinned. "I wasn't sure that you might hit me if I did that."

"Well, it's not like you're Damon."

"Ah, I wondered when you would bring that up."

"I'm not bringing it up. And come on. I still can't believe that he did that, purposely separating us all these years, hiding what he felt for me."

"It's good that he did. Like I said, we spent a lot of years doing a lot of things, and we fought for the right people, but, when everything blows up, it has a way of realigning what your real priorities are."

"Well, I'm hardly his priority."

"Maybe you are now," Terk suggested, with all seriousness. They hit the traffic light which magically changed with the crosswalk sign, not interrupting their stride.

She nodded. "That's another thing I've never understood about you."

"What?"

"How all the damn streetlights always change in your favor."

"Well, I don't know about *always*," he said, "but it does make for expediency."

"So you did do it!"

"Sure." He shrugged. "Easiest thing ever."

"Even when we were driving, I noticed that we never hit a single stoplight, ever."

"Well, stop *signs* I can't really do anything about." He chuckled. "But the traffic lights are a piece of cake."

She wondered at the ease of his movements as they walked on. Then she realized that six, maybe eight other people were around them. "It really is easier for you in a crowd, isn't it?"

"Not necessarily. This is easier, yes, because I can pull bits and pieces of their energy toward us, using them to help shield us, but, at the same time, I have to deal with their bits and pieces of energy."

She pondered that for a long moment. "I wish I knew more about what you did."

"We were always so busy that we never really had time for that, did we?"

"Not only did we not have time for that, it seemed like we barely had time to breathe," she stated. "Part of me was relieved that they were shutting down the team because I just needed a break, if you know what I mean."

"Absolutely," he replied quietly. "We all were in the same boat there. And then *this* happened."

"And you really have no idea what's going on with that Celia woman, do you?"

"No. I really don't," he admitted, "but believe me. I will find out. In the meantime, she's still out cold and healing. She had been badly beaten and is in rough shape."

"And yet the baby is still—" She broke off that thought.

"Yeah, she's still pregnant," he confirmed.

"Well, that doesn't surprise me," she muttered. "Any

offspring of yours will be tough as nails."

He burst out laughing again.

"You know, I don't think I've ever heard you laugh quite this much," she noted in surprise.

"Well, we haven't spent all that much time together and definitely not much off time."

"Is this off time?" she asked in a wry tone.

"Not really but, at the same time, I'm not sure I'll ever dedicate the same amount of time and energy to work like I have been."

"No," she agreed. "Plus the research was something that you were very addicted to."

He looked down at her, a strange look in his eyes. "What? I'm not sure that would be the word I would use."

"Well, you should," she murmured, "because you never let up on it. You were always trying to push the limits and to do more. If *addictive* doesn't work, how about *compulsive* or *obsessive* or maybe just *workaholic*."

"All of the above, most likely." He nodded. "Good call."

"Good call on what?"

"Well, both you and my brother have mentioned that maybe I need to get out of the industry."

"But then what?" she asked. "You have a very unique skill set. I'd hate to see it go to waste."

"I know, and I'm not sure what I'll do about that."

"Well, it's not like you must make a decision right now," she noted. "Especially when you'll be a family man soon." At that, she felt him stiffen beside her. "Sorry, that wasn't meant as a joke. I was serious."

"How does one become a family man of an offspring you didn't know about?"

"The same as anybody else," she stated. "Every father

becomes a father before he finds out about it."

When he looked at her in amazement, she shrugged. "Well, think about it. The woman always finds out first, unless you happen to be in the doctor's office at the same time that the news is broken. The father will always be the one who finds out second, and so it's always the same issue. You find out whether you like it or not. Whether you were looking forward to it or not. Whether this was a dream of yours or not. You find out, and you figure it out from there. It's just, in this case, you might have actually found out first."

"I've wondered about that. I don't know if she even knows."

"Or if she was being tortured because of you," she murmured.

"God, I would hope not," he replied. "To even think of what that woman went through makes me sick."

"And you probably know what she went through, don't you?"

"I do," he confirmed quietly. "And, no, I'm not sharing, so don't even ask."

"God, I don't want the details. I have enough nightmares already."

He nodded. "We all do. There is actually a technique to get rid of them, or at least keep them under control so you aren't impacted as badly."

"I don't know if that's even possible."

"It's not only possible, it's mandatory," he stated, "like in Celia's case. So I have blocked some of the harsher aspects of her torture. However, it's also mandatory that you don't ever completely forget because you can't afford to let people get at you the same way. Also you can't forget these times because you learn from them, because it keeps your humanity in place. It reminds you that shitty people are in the world, but also really good people are out there too," he murmured.

"Like your brother."

"Like my brother." He nodded. "And the team he works with."

"You know something? I find it odd that you, your whole team even, who have seen so much of the shitty parts of life, still trust all those people."

"I do, as they trust me. Like to let them know if there's anything amiss when they are out on missions."

She gasped. "Oh, that explains a few things."

He looked at her in surprise.

"Every once in a while, you zoned out in front of us, and sometimes what you were saying didn't make any sense. I often thought you were talking about drinks or something because you would talk about *ice*."

At that, he laughed. "Well, as much as I shouldn't be laughing at that," he admitted, "it's kind of funny because that's Levi's partner. Ice and I talked all the time. However, it is very disconcerting to consider that I was zoning out while people were around me," he murmured, obviously worried.

"Maybe," she replied, as they stepped inside the mall, and she took a deep breath, realizing that they were far safer in a public place like this. "The thing to remember is that you also knew you could trust us."

DAMON QUICKLY SENT out a barrage of texts.

Tasha immediately got back to him, saying they were in the mall across the road because Terk had insisted they leave due to dangerous probes at home. Damon was getting the same mental message. Immediately he shut off the phone, slipped against the concrete wall, and went silent. Instinctively he sent out an alert, asking Wade for tracking. Within seconds he realized what he'd done—Wade was one of the team members who was down, although he was recovering faster than the others but not enough. Yet if anybody out there could find another energy around Damon and track somebody breaching their security, it was Wade. Swearing softly under his breath, Damon then heard a faint voice in his head.

I'm here, Wade replied. *I'm here.*

"Shit, shit, shit," Damon muttered. "No, don't. Somebody's here. We're under attack. Get out of here!" And he tried to block out Wade. Injured, Wade was already vulnerable to attack. "They can trace you, dammit. Don't."

No, I can trace them, Wade responded, his voice getting stronger.

No, dammit, Damon whispered in his head, *they'll find you and track you back.*

I've got up a shield, Wade explained, his voice calm and gaining strength. *Just like we have to trust that you're doing what you can do*, he argued, *you have to trust me.*

I can't have you hurt any more, he stated. *We've got enough guys in bad shape already. The last thing we want is somebody else down.*

I may be down, but I'm not out, Wade snapped, and his voice was hard and determined. *I've got the signature. Actual spores. They haven't made it inside. They're on the outside of the building.*

Interesting, Damon murmured. *Can you track it?*

Yeah, I'm tracking it already. Looks very much like it's—he stopped his voice hesitant—*I think they found the warehouses, but I'm not sure how.*

What do you mean?

Well, I don't have any entrance or exit point where they entered.

Did they come in with a large group maybe?

Let me go take another look, he added. *Unfortunately I'm weak, as you know.*

I just assumed you shut him down, but maybe you can tell me if he's still here before you go.

He's gone. He tracked around the warehouse, but he couldn't find what he was looking for.

Well, that's a good thing. Terk and Tasha left to go to the mall.

That's smart, Wade agreed. *But you guys are definitely being hunted. Nobody's there now. You're safe at the moment. I'll try to keep note of the spore. I've attached a tracker to it, in case it comes close. I hate to say it, but I'm out.* And, with that, Wade's voice faded away.

"Shit," Damon whispered. But feeling better, he picked up his phone and called Terk. Quickly he explained what happened. "Wade says it's safe now."

"Okay, we're coming back again, and we picked up a few groceries."

"Of course you did. Tasha's doing by any chance?"

Terk chuckled. "Yeah, she does eat, doesn't she?"

"I think it might be stress eating."

"I don't care what you think," Tasha called out. "A girl has to eat."

"Fine. You guys come on back. I'll check the monitors

that we set up around the building and see if I find any-thing."

"Well, if our would-be intruder was just distant view-ing," Terk stated, "we won't see anything."

"I know, but I'm worried they may have picked up on you guys. So track carefully on your way back."

"We're shielded," Terk replied.

"I hear you, but if they're watching—"

"I know, but we can't wait for darkness. I've got just about enough energy to get back."

"Okay, I'll set up a perimeter guard."

And, with that, he hung up and stayed at the door, send-ing energy circulating around and around in a vibrating motion. He would have to open up a doorway to let in Terk and Tasha, but that was just part of it. He could do very little else with transmitting energy, except things like this. He could transmit messages. He could transmit all kinds of stuff. But, if nobody was around to receive it, the energy just wobbled and bounced back and forth, and that's exactly what he was doing now. He stood here, sending energy to himself. And he had set up an energy vibration level that was hard for anybody to trace.

He could sense them approaching too.

Soon Terk knocked on his mind. *We're here.*

Damon immediately stopped sending the energy. Feel-ing the vibration, he turned, opened the door, and they bolted inside. He immediately slammed it shut and set the energy moving again. Then he detached himself from it. "That should keep going for several hours or so," he stated, "but I'll have to reinforce it after that."

Terk nodded at the groceries in his arms. "Dinner."

Damon rolled his eyes, then looked at Tasha, staring at

him, her eyes wide open, and her pupils gone black.

He opened up his arms, and she rushed into them. He closed his arms securely around her and whispered, "You're safe."

She leaned back. "*I'm* safe?" She raised her voice in outrage. "What about you? You turned off your tracker."

He nodded. "And you can turn it back on again now."

"I will, and, if you ever try something like that again, … *ugh* …" she murmured, leaving the empty threat hanging.

He grinned, kissed her on the forehead. "What's this about food?" He looked back and forth between the bags that Terk held and the woman under his arm and asked, "Do you do anything but eat?"

"Are you saying I'm fat?"

"Are you kidding? You haven't got any body fat to spare." He shook his head. "I've often worried that you were anorexic."

She snorted, grabbed one of the bags from Terk's hands. "You don't know what you're talking about."

"Well, I hope not." Damon frowned. "I would hate to think that you had an eating disorder."

"The only eating disorder I have," she said, "is that there's not enough food when I'm hungry. I've always had a very high metabolism, and I can go through calories like nobody else."

"We've noticed," he quipped, but the return to light teasing was a joy. He looked over at Terk and asked, "You doing okay?"

"I am, but I—" He stopped, shrugged. "Well, you know. I was burning down, trying to keep this place protected in darkness while searching."

"And you've still got healing lines into all the team?"

He nodded. "But honestly, Brody worries me at the moment. He's in the worst shape, and he doesn't seem to be accepting any of my energy."

Damon sucked in his breath. "I hope not. I really don't want to lose anyone else."

"I know. None of us do. Maybe in some ways he prefers it. But he's on a 100 percent burnout. I'm not sensing any energy around him at all, except the tiny flat white aura stuck up to his body. And even then, the cord is fading."

"Shit." Damon glared at Terk. "Is there nothing you can do?"

"I'm doing it all." Terk sighed. "That's why I can't do much else. I can't do my usual channels because I'm funneling all the available energy I have to him. And it sucks because, at the end of the day, it's still not enough."

"Can I help? What about the others?" Damon asked.

Terk frowned. "You said you heard from Wade?"

Damon nodded. "Yes, and I told him to get his ass out of my head and to use the energy to heal, but he said he was doing better. Although tracking the spore, logging it in, then putting the tracker on it again so he'd recognize it later, all wore him out, so he's gone and crashed."

"Good," Terk muttered. "We all need food, and we all need rest." He looked at the bag in his hand. "Let's go eat."

They opened up the second room, and Terk put down his bag of food. Tasha immediately snatched it closer to her, opened it up, brought out the dishes, and looked at Damon. "I hope you like curry."

"I eat anything when it comes to food for energy," he replied calmly. "But it just so happens that I adore curry."

She handed him a takeout container heaped with rice on the bottom, vegetables in the middle, and a spicy chicken dish on top.

He looked at it and nodded. "This smells heavenly."

"Just because we're constantly under attack and in danger doesn't mean we shouldn't eat well," she stated, as she took another container and handed it to Terk. "You wanted beef, right?"

"I did." He nodded and sat down and proceeded very methodically and forcefully to eat, clearly intent on getting the entire meal down in short order.

CHAPTER 12

WHEN SHE WAS halfway done, Tasha looked at Terk and asked, "Are you actually enjoying what you're eating?"

"It doesn't matter if I am or not," Terk murmured. "I need to recharge, and, in order to recharge, I must have sustenance." He finished his meal, looked at the other two, and said, "I need to go crash."

"I'll be right after you." Damon nodded. "We're okay for the moment, since we have safeguards up."

"I'll stand watch," she offered immediately.

The two of them looked at her, shared a glance, and then shrugged.

"Because of the safeguards in place it's probably fine," Damon nodded. "So you can do first watch." And he went right back to shoveling food into his face.

She ate at a much slower rate. She did eat a lot, and she'd always known that, but it was a little more uncomfortable to have it be noticed all the time. It typically wasn't obvious because she didn't spend every waking moment with someone, but, in this scenario, well, it was pretty hard to hide. She watched as Damon ate and noted, "I hope you're at least enjoying it."

He nodded. "I am. It's really good. One question though," he said. "Why did you choose chicken for me?"

"Instinct."

His eyebrows shot up.

She shrugged. "Anytime we ever ordered sandwiches, you'd always go for roasted chicken. So I figured it was probably a safe bet."

"It is a safe bet, but, just for future reference, I love beef too. Hell, really not much I don't like."

"Good. For the record, I can't stand eggplant."

He stared at her. "Those purple-looking things?"

She nodded and smiled.

"I'm not sure I've ever had them," he noted.

"You probably have and didn't even know it." She shrugged. "I've always found them completely tasteless."

"Like a zucchini, huh?"

She smiled. "Those at least you can grill or roast, and they have some taste."

"I imagine people who love eggplant would say the same thing," he added.

"Maybe." He got up, and she watched as he stumbled. "Are you okay?" she asked in a low tone.

He nodded. "I am. You've seen this before though, I'm sure."

"I have, just not quite this bad." In fact, she hadn't seen Terk this bad either.

Damon made his way to the bathroom, and, when he came out, his face had been scrubbed, teeth brushed, and hair combed. He'd probably feel better if he had a shower.

"Do you have energy for a shower?" she asked.

He shook his head. "No, not until I wake up."

He walked over to his bed, and she swore to God that Damon was asleep before he even hit the mattress. While they did have three beds now, only two would be in use at one time. And, with the two of them down, gently snoring, an odd silence surrounded her. It was almost like no sound at all. She couldn't hear the sounds on the street, which she could last night. She couldn't hear anything. Curious, she got up and wandered over to a wall, placing her ear against it, but all sound was completely muffled. She didn't know if it was due to their safeguards or whatever energy Damon was running or something that even Wade might be doing.

The fact was, these men did things that seemed to come straight out of sci-fi or horror novels. She also understood that they had trained intensely for this. Terk had found them with something, some ability, then taught them how to hone it until it was almost a weapon in itself. That's what the whole superspecial ops program had been about. Distinct senses, tracking people, energy barriers, communications, all of the above and more.

She'd been amazed, and yet life had been so damn busy, and she wasn't kidding about that. She had no way to even analyze what they were doing, and, when she went home and crashed at nighttime so exhausted, she didn't want anything to do with it. Besides, at that time, anything she did have to do with it always came back to the fact that the man she was falling in love with didn't give two hoots about her.

She walked over to their makeshift coffee bar, put on some coffee, and, when the first cup was brewed, went back to her computers to check on all the searches she had running. Then she checked the news to see if the body in the truck in the parking lot had been found. It had, and that was good, and the news showed the man's face, asking for anybody who could identify him. She snagged a picture of the face, set it up for facial recognition, then sent it through one of her programs.

On a whim, she also sent it through the defense department programs, looking for anybody in their world who might have the same facial features. The news didn't say anything about how he died, only that he was found in the back of a stolen vehicle in the parking lot of an office building that had been closed for the day. Which coincided perfectly with everything that Damon had said.

It didn't make her feel any better because it was still another dead body. And she knew it was one of the other guys, one of the bad guys, and could very well have been the man who went after Wilson. At that thought, she opened the facial recognition software and started running all the images she had from the cameras at Wilson's and Mera's apartments.

With that running, she sat back and sipped her coffee, as she looked over at the two men. They were both sound asleep, and neither had moved. Both as still as logs, yet she sensed a weird alertness about them, as if somehow they still had some sensory advantage going on that would signal them if an attack came. It made her wary about getting too close to them while sleeping.

She figured she would just stay where she was and keep working. The paths to the bathroom, the coffeepot, and the food was clear, so she would let the two of them do what the men did best. When her computer beeped twenty minutes later, she looked over to see a photo side by side on the screen with the one she'd been scanning. And, sure enough, the dead man had been photographed outside of Wilson's apartment building, caught by a traffic cam. She shook her head slowly, as she looked at it. "You son of a bitch, you're the one who killed him."

With that knowledge, all her sympathy for him disappeared. "Well, you got what you deserved, asshole."

Then she hunted through the images from Mera's area, and, sure enough, there was a match for the dead asshole again. At two for two, she was pretty damn sure the dead asshole was also the one who had shot up her apartment, so she set it up to see if she could find any match near her place.

When the search came up empty, she frowned.

"I really don't like the idea of a second guy involved at this stage," she muttered. That would just suck. But not a whole lot else she could do. Except she sent her system running through the city to see if she could track the first killer's vehicle and his face and start charting where he'd been and what he'd done all that day.

It took her an hour and a half to get a connecting pathway, as she watched the vehicle come close to her apartment, about four blocks away, and she wondered if that had been close enough for him or if he was a secondary part of this. Maybe a backup or something. She didn't know, but, after that, he headed off to a shopping mall or possibly a restaurant or hotel. She kept the map up on the side and started to run the hotel registrations, looking for a sign-in around the same time that he had arrived in the area. And there it was, Peter Boswell out of Maryland.

"So, what are you doing over in Paris, idiot?"

She kept following his facial recognition hits as he checked out, only to realize that he checked back into another hotel on the other side of town, but then never showed up. Well, the hotel got paid, but they sure as hell didn't have to worry about cleaning a room or room service. The previous night he'd had steak, baked potato, and a bottle of wine. She stared at the effrontery of the man with such self-assurance, after killing one and injuring a second, to sit there and order such a meal. Worse, since he no doubt believed he'd killed Mera and Tasha too.

"Well, I hope it was your last supper," Tasha muttered.

She left everything up on one of the monitors for the guys to see when they got up. She checked the street cams tracking this guy's traffic patterns, trying to determine if anybody else had been in his vehicle.

"So, who the hell killed you?" she murmured to herself, wishing somebody else had been with him. Perhaps she could see someone else on the hotel camera. It took her a while to hack in, but, once she did, she couldn't see anybody but him on them. He was talking on the phone as he headed in though. She checked the registration and realized he'd actually left a phone number. She quickly found her way into Peter's phone records and tracked it down to see who he was calling.

She sucked in her breath when she saw it. "Bingo! Son of a bitch."

DAMON WOKE UP, hearing Tasha muttering to herself and arguing about food. When an alarm beeped obnoxiously, he shook his head, bolted to his feet, and cried out, "What the hell is that?"

But she was also racing for her keyboards. "It's an internal alarm. I set it up in case anybody tried to hack in."

He raced over to her side to see her shutting down programs. "Do you know where he's trying to get into?"

"Well, they're shutting down our access to the government sites," she complained balefully, as she stomped on the keys in a panic, trying to evade what was happening.

Damon could do absolutely nothing but stand here and watch. He glanced over at Terk, but he wasn't even disturbed by the alarms. "How is it he can sleep through all that racket?" he muttered.

"Because he's not sleeping," she explained. "You should know that."

"I do," he agreed, "it's just I'm surprised that the alarms didn't jolt him back out again."

"When he focuses, he's like a bloody laser," she muttered. "Absolutely nothing affects him."

"Well, I'm not sure about that either," he argued quietly. "Everything affects him, likely way too much."

She kept pounding away on the keyboards, and the siren suddenly stopped.

"So does that mean that they got what they wanted or that you got them out of there?"

"Both," she snapped. "They're out. They're gone, and I've locked them out, but they got in, and I'm not sure how." She buried her hands in her face and groaned. "God." She dropped her hands and raised her head. "I've got my work cut out for me now, trying to figure out how they got in."

"Where did they get to?"

"Oh shit," she said, working away on the keys.

He wanted to ask her more questions, but this was definitely her field. As she worked over the keys, she made magic happen on the screen. Suddenly faces popped up.

"What's that?"

"Something for you to peruse while you're waiting on me," she replied. "That's your dead guy, and I confirmed he was likely the one who killed Wilson and shot Mera," she murmured. "And that's everywhere he went the day he was killed and where he stayed the two nights."

Amazed, Damon studied the pathway she had back-tracked on this guy and realized that he had been cocky enough—or at least comfortable enough—to have gone about living his life, not worrying about retribution. When the second team of killers had come after Peter, they had come from behind, and Peter had no warning.

"They completely blindsided him," Damon murmured.

"Well, if you hire a killer, and you want to make sure there are no loose ends, you've got to make sure you're good at taking out your killer," she stated. "Otherwise you're the one who'll end up fried."

"True enough," he muttered. "But I don't think this guy had a clue that he would be next."

"Do they ever?" she murmured, as she continued to pound away on the keys.

"I don't know." Damon shrugged. "I'm putting on coffee. Do you want some?"

"Hell yeah," she snapped. "I'll need an entire pot now."

He winced, then walked over, made a fresh pot of coffee, and stretched, hating the way he'd been startled into wakefulness. And then he went back to studying the tracks of the dead killer. "It's not like he necessarily even tried to hide where he was."

"No. I just don't think he had the slightest idea that he could be next."

"But he also didn't seem to think that we were on to him or that we might follow him."

"And why is that?"

"I think because they believe anybody with any abilities is dead." He shook his head. "And the only way to know that ..." he murmured.

She looked at him. "How though? Did they see every-body's dead body? Assumed everybody was gone? Were they told everybody was gone? Possibly incorrectly? Just like I'm sure they think that I'm dead too."

He nodded slowly. "That's possible as well," he agreed. "None of this is good news though."

"It's excellent news if it means that we still have a little bit of a window to hide in."

He laughed. "I keep forgetting that you're a major part of the team."

"Hell no, I'm not," she argued. "I'm the scaredy-cat apparently. I would just as soon run away and hide."

"But you wouldn't want to spend the rest of your life hiding."

"No," she agreed, "and that's why I'm here. I'm also damn pissed about Mera and Wilson. This Peter is the asshole who took out Wilson. I know it. And the fact that he's dead now too makes me angry all over again because I don't get a chance to kick his ass."

At that, Damon burst out laughing. "You deal with what you got to deal with on the computers right now," he said. "I'll study this for a while and see what I can come up with."

"Good. I hope you can find something," she stated. "I've been studying it, and, although it tells us where he went, it doesn't tell us who he connected with. Oh—except for this." She brought up the last screen she'd been working on when the alarms went off.

He leaned forward and asked, "Who the hell is that?"

"Well, our guy Peter was making phone calls throughout the day. So, I hacked into the phone records, and this is one call he made over twenty times. Unfortunately," she said, as she clicked on a couple buttons, "this is where the number ends."

"Oh, Christ, the defense department." Damon groaned.

"Yep," she confirmed, "so I think Terk is right. Our own government tried to kill us."

"It doesn't mean he was doing it on behalf of the government though," Damon noted. "We have to watch making assumptions."

"What do you mean?"

"It could be Peter went rogue," he admitted. "I hate to say it, but it's not that uncommon for somebody in the government to go bad on their own and to get paid off by these foreign governments to target our own."

"Jesus. That's just wrong on so many levels." She stared at Damon in shock. "We do this work to protect our own, not to sacrifice them."

"In this case, he obviously warrants looking into, but that—"

Just then another tab on her screen started flashing.

She brought it up and explained, "Well, this is a search I did on Peter, once I got his name. So let's see how well that worked." She tapped the screen, and there it was. "Deceased, as you can see, this morning."

"Technically, depending on the time frame of the report's origin, last night, in that car park. Yet this says he was shot execution style in the head at home. Well, somebody is definitely cleaning up," he muttered. "So now the question is, who hired him, who killed him, and how do we track Peter's life?"

"Well, at least it gives me somebody's life to open up," she stated. "I was starting to get more than pissed because I didn't have any avenues to move on."

"You've done a hell of a lot of work already," he said in

admiration. "You've always been great at ferreting out information on these guys. Good job."

"Well, that's why I get the big bucks," she replied in a mocking note. "Unfortunately I didn't realize it was a death sentence at the same time. So apparently I'm just as stupid as these guys."

"No." Damon shook his head. "I would hate to have you think that. I don't think any of us would think we were stupid."

"But here we sit, looking for betrayal within. And is there even a chance it's not from within?" she asked, pivoting to shoot him a hard glance.

"Of course there is. We don't even know who this guy was talking to."

"No, not *yet*."

And she spoke with such emphasis on the word that he grinned, walked back to the coffeepot, and poured them each a cup. She was doing something. Terk was doing something, and now Damon was the one feeling like he couldn't do much. What he could do though was check the shield he had going outside.

It had to have worn down by now, and he sincerely hoped it wasn't completely gone, in which case it would take a ton of energy to get back up again, energy he really didn't have yet. He looked over at Terk, and, although the energy humming around him was steady and pulsing strong, it wasn't as full up as it normally was. Damon was getting worried about Terk expending too much energy in too many different directions and, therefore, being ineffective in all of them. But Damon also knew that talking to Terk wouldn't do any good.

"He's unnerving like that, isn't he?" she asked.

Damon looked over at her to see she had pushed her chair back, stood, and was even now studying their boss. "It is, but it's also reassuring in a way."

She looked at him. "I hadn't thought of it like that."

"Well, you should, because he's very good at what he does, and this is his 'into emergency mode' look."

"Into emergency mode?" she repeated, shaking her head. "Somehow it doesn't quite seem that way."

"Ah, it's just a paradigm shift," he explained. "Look at what's happened to us. He's just trying to protect as many people as he can."

"And how does he make that decision?" she asked quietly.

"Unfortunately it'll be based on expediency. Who he can save and who is too far gone, and it's a decision that I don't wish on him. Chances are, he won't break down and make a decision. He'll try to keep everybody alive. But he isn't God, and he can't make those determinations."

"It's not fair though, is it?" she murmured.

"Not at all, but what will we do about it?"

The coffee had his mind churning with all that had just happened and the information she dug up. It was actually massive. He stood to stretch a bit, when she made a crow of satisfaction.

"Got that little bugger trying to hack into my system."

"Did you find out who it was?"

"Nope, but I found his digital signature, and I'm tracking it back," she said. "And I've reopened access to the government databases."

"Is that smart?"

"Smart or not," she determined, "we need the information that I can get out of those sources. Even just like this right now, it's important. We wouldn't have to access this if we didn't find him in there."

"In other words, we need it."

"Yes," she agreed, "we have no chance without it."

"How long do we think it'll be before you track this guy back?"

"I don't know. He's sophisticated, and he's good, so it could take me days."

"Which is not what we want to hear."

"Nope, we don't."

"What worries me is if this hacker guy is just another hired gun, like our killer Peter, or if this hacker is part of their team. Like you are part of ours. Kinda makes me think they really are as good as we are."

She patted his hand, then lowered her voice quite a bit and added, "When I had time during the night, I also did a little more."

"Like what?"

She shot him a look. "I started hunting for Celia."

"And?" he asked, his voice sharp but low. "Anything?"

She shook her head. "No, so either she's operating under a different name, a nickname even, or a code name that she was given maybe."

"It's the name Terk used for her."

"So, maybe that's the name she thinks of herself as— potentially." Tasha raised an eyebrow. "There are a lot of reasons I'm not finding the name. Anyway, so far I haven't tracked down who she is or where she's from."

"According to Ice, Celia's fingerprints aren't showing any hits either."

"So, where the hell did this woman come from?" Tasha shook her head as she yawned. "It's pretty strange that, *A,* these bad guys found her. *B*, that they would use her. And, *C*, that she was even there for them to snatch."

"But we also don't know anything about it, so we have to reserve judgment," Damon noted.

"Like hell," she replied almost viciously. "We need answers, and we need them now."

After a moment, he asked, "Are you okay?"

"Sure." She shrugged. "But I didn't show you something else that I think you need to know about."

He looked at her in surprise.

She nodded got up, walked over to his side. "Take a look at this."

Her shirt was covered in blood.

"Where's that coming from?" he asked, immediately lifting her shirt, checking to see where her wound was.

"It's not mine," she said. She turned to look at Terk. "It must have come from him, when he had his arm wrapped around me, while he was trying to keep me under his shield of protection," she murmured. "That has to be the way I got it."

He stared at her in shock, then turned to look at Terk. Even as he did, Terk's eyes opened wide. "Terk," he demanded, "are you hurt?

"It's nothing," he said in a low tone.

"Jesus, man. You know that even the smallest of injuries can end up being a huge headache for us."

"It could be," Terk agreed, "but it isn't this time." Slowly, and using the wall for assistance, he pushed himself vertical and yawned at the same time. "I'll sure be glad when this is over, but I don't think it'll happen anytime soon."

"I don't want to hear that," Tasha cried out. "I've worked all night trying to find information."

"Yeah, you were supposed to let us know when it was time to change the watch," he noted. "That's the problem with having green people on watch. They don't follow the same rules the rest of us do." Terk glared at her.

She glared right back. "No," she argued. "You're burnt out. You were injured, and you needed to be looked after. So, whether you like it or not, tough guy, that's what I was doing."

Damon almost choked when he listened to her reaming out Terk. Very few people had the balls to do so, but she was apparently one of them, and Damon appreciated that. He would go toe to toe with Terk himself, but sometimes it just wasn't worth the fight. "Let me check out the wound," Damon said, walking over to stand in front of Terk. Damon put his hands on his hips and glared at his friend.

"It's nothing really. Just forget it."

"Oh, hell no. None of that."

Terk sighed. "You're really making a fuss over nothing."

"If it was nothing," Damon noted, "you wouldn't be arguing about letting me look at it."

At that, Terk glared and lifted his shirt, so they could see a long funky scrape along his side.

"How'd you get that?" he asked.

Terk shrugged. "Honestly, I'm not sure."

"That's actually a little more concerning," Damon said, as he pulled the shirt back up and glanced at it. "It needs cleaning and will probably be okay, but what I don't get is where you got it from. It looks like you scraped against something at a hard angle."

"I know. Honestly, I don't remember where I got it."

"Are you getting blackouts again?" he asked in a low voice, low enough that hopefully Tasha didn't hear him.

Terk averted his gaze.

"Goddammit, Terk," Damon growled. "You know this isn't the time to hold back information. We can't do our job if you're keeping stuff from us."

"I can't hold back what I don't know," he replied, with a note of humor.

But Damon wasn't impressed. "That's bullshit, and you know it. Come on. A first aid kit is over here."

"Shit, if I'd have known that was there," he muttered, "I could have taken care of it before."

"Oh, that's crap, and you know it. You're the one who ordered the damn thing. Seems like there's always something about our work that requires it," he said, with his own note of humor.

"Isn't that the truth?"

Even as Damon cleaned the wound, Terk didn't appear to be bothered. He was just yawning and waiting patiently for Damon to be done. Damon lowered his voice and asked Terk, "How is everyone doing?"

Tasha turned at that question and asked, "Yes, how is everybody doing?"

Terk stared at her steadily. "Most are fine."

"Most?"

"Most," he confirmed. "Obviously not everybody is out of the woods yet."

She frowned. "You're saying Brody won't make it, aren't you?"

"He is tough, and he's got as much of a chance as anybody, but it's not looking particularly good." Terk took another deep breath and added, "I have some other bad news to deliver."

She looked at him in surprise. "What? How much bad

news are we supposed to absorb?" she snapped.

"One more at least." He looked over at Damon. "It's Mera. She died this morning."

Tasha bolted to her feet, crying out, "What? No! No. She was safe. What do you mean, she's *dead*?"

He nodded. "I haven't gotten official notice. All I can tell you at the moment is that her life forces have stopped."

Tasha stared at him, trying to process the information, as Damon realized just how much Tasha was having to deal with. Normally these conversations would have been kept out of her range. But there was really no way to protect her from all that was going on right now.

"Did she die on her own?" she asked.

"I highly doubt it," Terk answered quietly.

"I didn't see anywhere else Peter could have been." She pointed to the map. "I followed his footsteps, tracked him through the city all day yesterday, right up to where he ended up at his first hotel, to the meal, to the phone calls he made." She then motioned over at the last person, a picture still up on the wall. "Including the government official that he was talking to five times on his last day."

At that, Terk's face hardened. "Well, I want to have a talk with him."

"Well, that's too damn bad," she snapped, "because, just like Mera, this guy is dead." He stared at her in shock; she nodded. "Yep. Our bad guys have been damn busy on their killing spree." She shook her head. "But where the hell does this ever stop?"

"It doesn't stop unless we stop them," Terk said. "Unfortunately that's part of the reason our department was created. We had to have a way to stop these guys, who just seem to be invincible."

"The trouble is they aren't invincible, and neither are you," she said pointedly, looking at the bandage that Damon had put on Terk's ribs. "And you need to remember that."

He smiled at her. "I'm glad you care," he replied in a teasing voice.

She rolled her eyes. "I do care. I also don't want to be left alone to face all this shit," she admitted. "If something happens to you, I'm totally screwed." And just enough spunk filled her voice that his grin widened.

"So, it's not about me at all," Terk noted. "It's all about you. Got it."

She raised both hands in frustration. "Don't you start pissing me off."

"But it's such fun," he quipped. "You react beautifully."

She groaned and slumped back in her chair. "I'm tired. I'm worn out. I've had a shitty night, and what was supposed to be a lot of really good information ended up in a dead end. Then we had a computer attack, and, even though I've got everything restored and have a bunch of traces going," she added, "I'm starting to fail."

Immediately Damon piped up. "Why don't you go to bed?"

"Well, wouldn't that be nice," she quipped, "but how in the hell am I supposed to do that when so much is going on?"

He could see the shimmer of tears in her eyes and realized that it wasn't so much that she was tired and worn out but that the news about Mera had hit Tasha hard. He walked over, wrapped his arms around her, and just held her close. She protested for a moment, then burrowed in, laying her head tucked up against his heart, a damn fine place for her as far as he was concerned. But he also knew he had a way to go before she would trust him, after deliberately keeping her at arm's length without acknowledging the attraction between them. "I'm sorry," he whispered.

"Me too." She nodded. "Apparently being sorry doesn't count for shit anymore," she muttered. "I just want these guys caught, and I want this over with."

"I don't know that we'll get both of those done anytime soon," he admitted. "Our focus right now is finding the ones who have been taking out our friends. Then we'll go from there."

"And that was something else." She pulled her head back, looked up at Damon and over at Terk. "Why was all of your team taken out one way and my team taken out another?"

"For the same reason that the Peter guy, who did your part of the team, was killed," Terk said in a quiet voice. "Fast and efficient and all were expendable. Too many cooks spoil the broth. So they just turn around and start cleaning up."

"Why is it that you guys in this business don't expect to be in that position where you're the ones getting cleaned up?" she asked with emphasis. "That's the part I don't get. How is it that we—or them—actually think we/they would be part of this forever?"

"I don't know," Damon replied, "and that's a good and valid question. If and when we get a chance to ask them, we will."

She snorted at that, pulled out of Damon's arms, and stated, "I'll go lie down." She walked over to her bed and crashed.

He watched, seeing her wrap her arms around her shoulders, aware of the pain in her stiff movements. He looked over at Terk and raised an eyebrow.

Terk nodded. "I think I'll go have a shower. I need to get back to the land of the living. Then we need to go over this information she dug up, which is huge, but I feel like something is in there we can utilize to find whoever took out our assassin here." And, with that, he headed into the bathroom.

With Terk out of the room for a bit, Damon walked over and sat down on the side of Tasha's bed. When she stiffened, he said, "It's just me. Terk's taking a shower. Are you okay?"

"Of course I'm not okay," she replied through her tears.

He pulled her upright, picked her up into his arms, and just held her gently while she bawled. When she finally slowed down the tears, she looked up at him, her huge eyes glistening, as she whispered, "Mera didn't do anything. She was already hurt. She was unprotected, and it wasn't fair."

"No, it isn't fair," he agreed, "and, after you have a nap, you can get busy tracking who and what may have been there."

She looked over at the computers, and he shook his head. "I'll get it started," he said, "but, if and when we come up with something, you can step in and go deeper."

She nodded. "Fine. Honest to God, I am really tired."

She pulled out of his arms without another word and curled up on the bed. He grabbed the blanket and laid it over her shoulders, tucking her in, so at least she'd be warm while she slept. After taking several long slow deep breaths, she crashed.

CHAPTER 13

WHEN TASHA WOKE, she felt a heart-heaviness rising from the deep dark depths. She hadn't realized how tired she was; adding that to the emotional exhaustion resulted in everything hurting, inside and out. As she lay here, she realized her body also felt this burden. She needed a good workout, something to relieve some of this stress. She heard a conversation going on around her, and it took a moment for her to register that something exciting was happening. She propped herself up on her elbow to see Damon at a computer, pounding away on the keys. "What's going on?" she asked, bolting to her feet.

"Tracking somebody from the visual software that you've got up at Mera's place."

"You mean, her killer?" Tasha asked in a hard voice.

"Yes," he said quietly, "quite possibly."

She walked over and said, "Let me." He hesitated, but she added, "Go, and I need food." She stated it in almost a preemptive manner, and he burst out laughing.

"Only because I know you're better at this than me," he noted, "and I'm damn good."

"Yeah, but you're not me," she replied quietly, as she sat down and started, her fingers flying over the keyboard. "Interesting," she muttered.

"What's interesting?"

"You're tracking it, but I don't think it's a real set of tracks."

"What do you mean?" Now both Terk and Damon crowded around behind her.

"I think we have somebody planting information in the software to throw us off. That's what that damn hacker was doing earlier."

"How the hell did you see that?"

She pointed to the IP addresses in the code running after it. "We've got fake avatars here."

"I don't understand that at all," Terk said. "Why would they do that?"

"Because they know we're hunting them, and, if they give us somebody, and then he turns up dead, we'll stop looking, won't we?"

"Maybe, do you think this guy now is dead?" Damon asked, frowning at Terk.

"No, not yet, but I think that he's next on the list. If you can get to him ahead of them, then it's a whole different story. We might actually prevent that hit, and we could get some answers."

She shook her head. "No guarantee that this guy will give us answers though," she said. "It doesn't seem like they want to talk much."

"Well, maybe if they see the bodies of the other henchmen."

"That's a different story maybe," she agreed. "Yet seems like a long shot. I don't know."

"You got an address?"

"Address, no. ... I do have coordinates though." She handed them off to Damon. She looked over at him and added, "But I want to come along."

"You can't be in two places at once," he stated. "Besides, it's probably a recovery mission."

She winced. "*Great.* Maybe you can get Merk to go take a look."

"I don't know where he's at now—but maybe."

Terk immediately picked up his phone and walked a distance away and asked, "Bro, where are you?" As he listened to the response, he turned back to them. "He's about a mile away from the location."

"Then maybe have him carefully go in," she suggested, "realizing it could be a trap, and he could be leading somebody back to his home base just by being there."

"We got it," Terk replied. "Merk does say thanks for being worried though."

She rolled her eyes at that. "How could I not be? We've already lost so many. I don't know him, but they've got Celia, so … and see if you can find a different name for her," she asked. "Because I can't track her with just that."

As Terk put his phone away, he looked at her. "Have you been trying?"

"Of course I've been trying," she replied in exasperation. "We need to know how this connects to everything."

"Yeah, I really would appreciate it if you could find something on her," he added quietly. "I suspect that she's as much a victim as I am in this, but I don't know that for sure."

"No, but, until then, we'll look at it that way," she stated, "because I think it's one hell of a shitty deal. For the mother and the baby."

"Yeah, well, I'm not feeling too great about it either," he confirmed.

She turned to look at Damon, only he wasn't in the

room. She bolted to her feet and raced to the next room, but he was gone. "Shit," she almost yelled. "He took off again without the tracker online."

"I know," Terk admitted quietly. "He'll go meet Merk, and he doesn't want anybody to track either of them to their home bases."

"Well, what's the point of having trackers if you don't use them?" She glared at Terk, mad that he let Damon leave like that.

Terk gave her a half smile. "Surely you haven't forgotten how much Damon's always hated having trackers."

"Since when is it optional?" she snarled at him.

"Hey, it just shows how much you care, so I thank you for that."

She shook her head. "Caring for you guys is a nightmare. Why would anybody want to?" she asked. "You take chances. You get yourself into dangerous scenarios, where nobody can help you, and you all will get your asses kicked, if not killed," she growled, as she sat back down at her computer.

"Why don't you try some food?" Terk suggested. "You sound hungry."

She stood and glared at him. He immediately pointed to the sideboard where all the leftovers were. She walked over and, still in a fury, built herself a huge plate and sat again at her computer.

"I'll just leave you alone for a while," he offered gently.

She didn't even growl back at him. It was probably a good thing because, what she wanted to say, she probably shouldn't say to her boss. But then again, she had to laugh at that because she could do nothing else. It's not as if she was getting paid for this assignment anyway. What she hopefully was doing was helping to keep them safe, so they could actually have a life when this was over. Although it appeared there was a pretty slim chance that would happen at this rate. Pissed, she sent Damon a message, telling him how she felt about his decision.

What she got back froze her in place, as she stared down at his message.

I love you too.

And all she could think about was whether or not he meant it. Or was he just being flippant, like they so often were? She studied the message and then forcibly put it away, so it wouldn't just sit there and taunt her. But all it did was mess with her head as she continued to question it, then realized she couldn't afford to let him sidetrack her. Yet isn't that exactly what he didn't want her doing for him, … tracking? She groaned, then settled back and proceeded to eat, plowing through the food in record time. That was unusual for her, as normally she could get the food she needed and enjoy it too.

When Terk's hand landed on her shoulder, she immediately stopped eating and looked up at him.

"Slow down," he said quietly. "Damon is fine."

She took a deep breath, let it out noisily, "Is that what's bugging me?"

He gave her a ghost of a smile. "Well, I could tell you how this will all go"—he paused—"but I think the journey is more special if you find out for yourself."

And, with that cryptic remark, he turned and headed back to his computer. She wanted to ask a million questions, but it's not as if he was up for giving even a single answer, much less one million. Now she really couldn't get Damon off her mind.

IT PROBABLY WASN'T fair that Damon had taken off without saying goodbye, but, with only the three of them, he was pretty well the one who needed to be out here. He also couldn't let Merk walk into anything too dangerous without a partner here on the ground with him. Merk was here helping them after all, and everybody needed backup, sometimes even Levi's team.

Damon raced over to the coordinates they'd been given. As he approached, he heard a voice inside his head. *Wade, what's up?*

He said, *Watch it.*

Wade, are you okay?

Not really, he muttered. *I feel like I'm being hunted still. And I don't know if that's an actual fact or if it's just paranoia setting in.*

It's something that we always have to watch out for.

I know, he agreed.

So what did you mean when you told me to watch out?

It feels like a trap, Wade stated.

Yeah, I don't have much choice though. We have to spring it.

Damn, I wish I was on my feet, Wade said.

How are you doing physically? Damon asked, as he studied the area hidden in the shadows. He'd left his vehicle a couple blocks away.

I feel like shit, but I don't think I've regained consciousness.

Damon had to stop and think about that. *Seriously? Do you really think you're unconscious?*

Well, I don't think I'm necessarily all there, he muttered.

And I know that probably doesn't make sense, Damon replied.

You know the stuff we do, he said. *It almost never makes sense*, but a note of laughter was in his voice.

You actually don't sound too bad, considering that you're likely still comatose.

Maybe, he replied, *but I don't feel great.*

No, of course not. You've pretty well been annihilated by some asshole.

Yeah, that's what it feels like, he agreed.

You got any hints on the trap?

It's the same spore I picked up outside the place you guys are staying. What is that anyway?

It's a warehouse among warehouses, Damon said.

Yeah, feels like something along that line.

If you get anything else, let me know. We've got Merk here too though, so make sure you're not mistaking that energy.

Merk? Merk? he repeated. *I don't feel like I know that name. Did you mean Terk?*

No, I don't. I mean his twin brother.

Oh shit, man. Levi's team is involved?

We didn't really have too many people we could call on, Damon replied, *so yeah.*

Well, they have a different energy too, he noted, *but I haven't worked with it very much.*

Enough to know it?

Not really, he noted. *I wish I could say yes to that but I really can't.*

Don't worry about it, Damon replied. *I've got this.*

Well, you must have some of it, he stated, *but I'm not kidding about it being a trap. And it feels like it's closing in on you right now. Man, you better move your ass.*

And, with that, Wade was gone, but Damon was already

on the run. He wasn't exactly sure who or what was after him, but nothing quite like this industry and the work they did to make him realize so many things were worse than a bullet. He pulled into a shadowy doorway and sent out a message to Terk. *You there?*

Terk immediately answered. *Yeah, what's the matter?*

Wade warned me it was a trap.

Shit.

Damon wasn't sure if it was *shit* because of what the message was or because of the fact that Wade was using his skills. *He also told me that he didn't think he was conscious.*

That gave Terk pause. *He was operating in a coma?* he asked, puzzled.

That's what he said, but I have no idea. Maybe you'll want to ask him yourself. Can you find out where Merk is?

Yeah, hang on.

Damon waited, feeling the same buzzing energy that Terk always used when he grabbed hold of your energy so he could take a look around.

He's up three blocks to the left.

Anything in between us?

Not that I see, Terk replied, *but I get Wade's feeling of something being off.*

"Of course something's off," Damon muttered. "Like I need this shit." But he slipped through the shadows, heading forward. *Do you want to tell your brother that I'm here?*

I already sent him a message that you were a few blocks away and to expect you in a few minutes.

Is he likely to shoot me in the process?

He hasn't yet, has he?

No, not yet, Damon said, *but I really don't want that handicap right now.*

You're good to go.

And, with that, he raced forward the last remaining bit. When he stepped into the next hiding spot, he wasn't alone. He stared at Merk. "Hey."

"Hey. What's this about a trap?"

Damon shrugged. "One of our team contacted me to say this was a trap. On a slightly bizarre sidenote, he also believes he's in a coma."

Merk stared at him for a long moment. "Jesus Christ, you're all nuts."

"Maybe, but it's what we do."

"And that's why I'm here," Merk said.

"Well, in truth," Damon corrected, "you're here because of your brother."

"Yes, that too, but also because he put out a call for help for your team. We know all about what teams are for, and we won't leave ours on the ground when help is required."

"Much obliged," Damon replied quietly. "This mess has been a FUBAR from the beginning."

"Unfortunately things seem to be getting worse all around these days."

"Your team too?"

"The cases are getting more complex. Some of the calls we get are from governments, almost panicked because they're in the middle of a coup and people are getting shot with absolutely no regard for innocent lives lost." He shook his head. "It seems like things have just gone to shit in a handbag."

"Sorry, I know that's hard enough to handle right now, but, when it's everywhere and when it feels like it's a losing battle, it becomes almost impossible." He saw a flash of light sweeping over Merk's face as Merk noticed it too and smiled.

"One thing at a time," Damon said, "and right now we need to find what the hell is going on up ahead. Let's follow where that light came from."

Merk said, "I'll do a reconnaissance visit to the left."

"Okay," Damon agreed, "I'll check out the right."

And, with that, Merk disappeared into the shadows.

Damon contacted Terk. *You brother has gone left. I'm heading to the right.*

Good enough, Terk replied, *I'll step outside away from the concrete and see if I can get a clear link.*

I hate to even have you do that, Damon replied. *That leaves her alone in there.*

She's working on the keyboard, he murmured, *and we each have to take chances.*

I wish to God you could see into the future with this shit to see if we'll make it.

And sometimes, Terk noted, *those kinds of answers aren't helpful.*

I know. We've seen that before too. But right now I could really use the vote of confidence suggesting that we'll make it.

Come on. It's who we are and what we do, Terk replied, with a bravado and a self-confidence that Damon didn't feel at the moment. *You'll be fine.*

I'll be fine if I'm dead or alive. I know that already, he said in exasperation, *but that doesn't tell me if she'll make it through this.*

And none of us can see that right now, and I haven't been invited to see it either.

Terk used wording like that sometimes, and it was frustrating. None of them could directly see the information that they wanted to see; it always came in dribs and drabs. Bits and pieces more often than not, frequently not very helpful.

I get it, Damon admitted, *but watch your back, and please don't take any unnecessary chances.* And, with that, he signed off and crept forward into the darkness. It didn't take long for him to come up against something that made his fingertips buzz. He sent Terk a message, saying, *We're up against something energetic.*

Terk sent a message back. *Yeah. I think it's similar to barriers you see all the time—or what you do yourself.*

Seriously? Damon tentatively opened up his own senses and pressed forward ever-so-slightly. It was exactly that. Somebody, a receiver and a transmitter, was sending the same signal around in a big loop, keeping whatever was inside well guarded.

The question was, what was inside?

Do we know what's in there? Damon sent back to Terk.

No, he paused, *but it feels … familiar.*

At that, his heart froze. *Jesus, like what kind of familiar?*

I don't know. Terk's voice was harsh. *Proceed with caution.*

I don't even know how I'm supposed to get through this. Damon sighed. Even he heard the lack of confidence he felt now, what with his special gifts at half power.

The same way you get through your own, Terk sent, humor in his words. *You join it.*

And, with that, Damon studied it and realized that was exactly what he would have to do. But he would have to hook in at the right time. He sent out his own energy, brought it up to the same vibration, then slowly let it blend in, pulling his energy around and around and around. He tried to see through to the other side, but he wasn't getting anywhere. Finally, when it was up to the same level, he stepped in, letting it go through and around him.

And, in his next step, he went to the other side. There he stopped at a door, but he didn't know what was on the other side of it, and he had no way of finding out. He hoped nobody had had any early warning of his arrival, but Damon had no way to know that either. He'd learned a lot working with Terk, but Damon had also come to gain a few of his own skills that he didn't know if Terk even knew about. And Damon would need everything he had to offer right now.

He shifted forward to the door, quickly unlocking it and stepping inside. He had a handgun in one hand, but he was armed with a fist in the other. He'd been a boxer a long time ago, and, at times, guns just didn't do the job.

As his eyes adjusted to the darkness inside, nobody was here, just a room with a couch and a desk and a laptop, but it was closed, as if nobody was even here. But then he spied another door off to the side. He crept forward and slid up, so he had his ear against the nearby wall. Then he sent out transmitted energy to see if he could hook on to whatever was happening on the other side.

When he was in the right position and with his energy working at full capacity, which was not the situation now, he could often hear what was happening on the other side of a closed door. Not like a remote viewing, which was a completely different thing, but almost as if he could pull that energy toward him, so he could decipher what was happening. On the other side, he heard a voice, like in the middle of a phone call.

"I know. I know." Then silence. "No, we got this," the man said. "I promise we've got it. They won't find us, and they sure as hell won't find this asshole I've got here."

At that, Damon's heart froze.

"He's in a coma. Why can't we just kill him? I swear to

God, it's just easier to shoot these guys. One bullet and he's gone. What do they call him? Wade or something?"

Damon's throat closed, as he thought about Wade, completely innocent and lying unprotected at the hand of another gunman. Damon sent out an urgent message, *Wade. Wade, can you hear me?*

What? came his groggy voice.

Any chance you can wake up?

I don't know, he replied. *Why?*

I'm hiding on the other side of a door, near somebody who I think has you captive. I'm not sure how that happened because I thought you were being protected, but no time to argue about that right now. The guy is on the phone now, trying to convince someone to let him just shoot you.

There was silence as Wade tried to gather up the energy to talk to Damon. *I don't know,* he whispered. *That'd be a shitty way to go.*

I'll go in, Damon told him.

Yeah, guns blazing again, Wade replied in a wry tone. *Make sure you don't have random bullets flying around, okay? I'm already a sitting duck.*

You have no idea. If there is anything you can do to assist right now, it would be helpful.

Outside of the fact that the energy is familiar again, Wade noted, *I can't say much.*

Familiar? Familiar how? Damon asked.

I don't know, man. I really don't know.

Damon stopped and froze at an ugly thought. *Wade, do you have any family?*

What kind of a question is that to ask? You know I do. I have a brother.

Yeah, and where was your brother working?

In Europe. Why?

Is this energy that kind of familiar?

After a moment of shocked silence, Wade asked, *Are you accusing my brother of holding me hostage and possibly wanting to kill me?*

I'm not accusing your brother of anything, Damon replied. *I can only tell you what I just overheard and what I think is happening on the other side of this door.*

Jesus. Wade paused. *I can't tell. Things are just so dull that I can't even tell you that much.*

That's fine, Damon said. *I need you to pull in all your energy as low and as deep as you can. Yes, bullets and all kinds of shit may soon be flying, but, if you can make a move so you're somewhat protected, lurching like a drunk or not, I'd appreciate it. Because, when I come in, unfortunately it'll be guns blazing.*

But no response came from Wade.

Wade, are you there, man? Come on. Talk to me. Talk to me. But Damon got nothing.

In the background he thought he heard a hard spit. His heart froze, as he kicked in the door and, with his gun at the ready, entered in a fury. And a man stood there, with a gun against a prone figure on the bed. Damon didn't have time to see if it was Wade.

When the gunman looked up, startled to see Damon suddenly appear, the gunman smiled. "I'll just shoot him right now," he taunted. "And I thought for sure you were a goner."

"Yeah, well, you didn't check," Damon replied.

"And that was my mistake. I get it," the gunman noted calmly. "But you can sure as hell bet I won't make another one."

"You already did. You had to go back and finish up your

other asshole's job and kill off poor Mera," he murmured. "Your local hire couldn't even be trusted to kill off three people in one night, could he?"

The guy's face twisted in fury, and then he calmed somewhat, as if realizing Damon was trying to rattle him. "Good help is hard to find." He shrugged. "But if you don't put down that gun, I'll blow your friend to bits."

"You blow my friend to bits, and I'll take you out," Damon stated, "no question. You're done. So which will it be?"

The guy stared at him. "You won't get any answers out of me."

"Well, at least I'll know that we took out one of the guys involved in this raid," Damon muttered. He studied the gunman for a long moment, stepping closer. "Jesus, he's your brother for crying out loud."

"What are you talking about?" the man asked in surprise, stepping back.

"Hands up," Damon ordered.

"I can still shoot him. Drop the gun and put your hands up."

"Do you think I don't know that you're Wade's brother? You think we haven't felt that same familiar energy?"

"Energy?" he asked, trying to deflect.

"Don't joke with me," Damon snapped. "Whoever put up that energy guard around this building knows a thing or two."

The guy beamed. "Yeah, I sure do." He shook his head. "And, yeah, it's my brother. Too bad my brother chose to work on the wrong side of the wrong team. I tried to get him to come my way a long time ago, but he wouldn't have anything to do with it. He had plenty to say about my choices in life though," he noted. with a shrug. "I never did understand that holier-than-thou personality."

"You think so?"

"Yeah, I know so."

And just then a moan came from the bed. The gunman looked down at his brother, startled, his trigger finger clenching, as Damon's gun fired, hitting the gunman's wrist. The gunman's own shot went wild as he jerked backward, dropping the gun and holding his injured hand. He stared at Damon in shock. "Jesus Christ. The least you could have done is killed me."

"Not happening," Damon replied, "unless you have somebody who'll do the job for you. But they won't do that until they know for sure that you're not dead yet."

He stared at him. "What are you talking about?"

"They're taking out everybody they can. Nobody is left alive. You're no different."

"No, that's not true," he argued.

"Yeah, it is. The first guy who hit our people was Peter Boswell," Damon stated. "He's dead now. Did you kill him?"

"I had to. He was a loose screw, and, besides, he didn't do the job."

"So you cleaned up, and of course our little government man has been taken out."

He frowned. "Bob?"

"That's a name I'm hearing first from your lips."

"Yeah, I used to work with him a long time ago. He's a dirtbag. But then some of those suits are. They get comfortable in their job and become mostly pencil pushers and don't even realize when you take over their log-ins and do all kinds of shit behind their backs."

"Somebody decided that Bob was a loose end."

He stared at him in shock. "He's dead? I thought you meant he was moved or fired."

"Yeah, he's dead," Damon stated, holding the gun on Wade's brother. "What else do you know?"

"I don't know jack shit"—he smiled—"except that you guys' days are numbered, and a pretty decent contract is on your heads. But it's already been accepted by another group."

"What group?"

"I don't know." He shrugged. "It's not like I've got the contract, so I don't give a shit."

"So who were you just talking to on the phone then … about shooting your own brother?"

"I wasn't talking to anybody." He gave Damon a flat stare.

"Liar. Absolute lies," Damon snapped.

"Well, if it's a case of lying, you might want to keep me alive, just for leverage."

"Why is that?"

"Because your home base that you thought was safe isn't safe," he explained, "and my brother was a backup trap just in case. But we've got her now, so if Wade lives or dies now, it doesn't matter."

"Her? Who are you talking about?" But in his heart Damon knew. "What have you done?"

"I was helping governments and helping myself at the same time. Nobody looks after us when we get old and gray."

"You don't need to be looked after when you're old and gray," Damon said bluntly. "None of you guys survive that long."

He stared at Damon, his face turning ugly. "Well, that female we missed the first time around, we don't have to worry about her anymore," he snapped. "Because she's the one we nabbed. And believe me that'll be a done deal before you ever get out of here."

Feeling his heart pound and hoping it was all lies and bravado, he sent a mental message to Terk. *Jesus Christ, you better have Tasha with you. This asshole says they've picked her up already.*

They have, Terk's voice hard and grim. *They already have.*

Damon immediately turned back to the gunman, who was already laughing at him. "Where are they taking her?"

"You'll have to find out," Wade's brother taunted. "I don't give a shit."

And, with that, Damon dove into the guy's mind, looking for whatever messages he was sending and receiving.

Immediately the man screamed in pain. "What are you doing? What the hell! Stop!"

"Like hell I'll stop," Damon snapped brutally. "Where is she?" He kept hunting through the guy's energy, looking for whatever messages he might have sent, realizing that the guy was stressed and exhausted, his mind a mess. "You haven't had a break at all, have you?" Damon noted. "You haven't had a rest."

But the guy was on his knees, his bloody hand holding his head as he screamed and screamed. "They're here."

"Jesus, they're coming here." And, with that, he gave a slight push, and the gunman collapsed unconscious on the floor.

Retrieving the man's gun from the floor, he walked over to Wade. *Terk, the kidnapper is coming here with Tasha. I'll need you and Merk whenever they get here. Wade's still unconscious, and the gunman here just happens to be Wade's brother.*

Shit. I'm already on the way, Terk sent, *and so is Merk. He's only minutes away.*

Well, he better watch it because, if anybody comes through that door without identifying themselves first, I'll kill them, Damon snapped. *No questions asked.*

CHAPTER 14

TASHA HAD HEARD Terk step outside, but she was working away on the keyboard, trying hard to track down that last asshole she had on a hook. Damon had done a hell of a job tracking him online, but she'd widened the search. When she heard a sound, she didn't even think about it. "Did you find out anything?"

But the voice that answered wasn't the one she expected. She spun and bolted to her feet, as a cloth was slapped over her face, and the last thing she saw was a balaclava-covered face standing over her as she went under.

Waking up—struggling, kicking, and fighting like crazy—a man at her side laughed. "Keep on fighting. It won't do you any good, but keep on fighting if you like."

She was tied up and wasn't going anywhere. She was also in a moving vehicle. She looked around, but a dark hood was over her eyes, and she couldn't see a thing.

"Good. At least that'll keep you a little bit calmer until we get to our destination," the man noted.

She tried to ask him where she was being taken.

"Oh, are you trying to talk? Well, if I thought you could actually be trusted, I'd be happy to talk to you," he muttered. "Doing so much mental work is a lonely job, but I don't get to talk to my victims that much. I just go in and kill them. Or, if I can't kill them, I go in and wipe their minds. Same difference to me. In your case, well, it'd be a whole lot more fun. We're trying to get the rest of your team and guess what? You're the bait." He laughed. "It's always a pretty woman because men are so predictable." He chuckled. "But it's good for us. Oh, that's right. You don't even know who *us* are. Well, that's because you guys are stupid and not very good at your jobs," he replied, still laughing. "Our hacker said your system was all too easy to get into."

Heart pounding, trying to ignore the fogginess in her brain and the pain in her body, Tasha waited, just listening, trying hard to pick up anything that would make sense or would help in some way. So far she found nothing of value. Except that she was being used as bait and moved to a new location, where they could try to draw in the men. Of course they would. Particularly Damon.

He would get pulled in and get hurt badly; she just knew it. She didn't have any basis for it, but she sent out messages immediately, telling the guys to sacrifice her and to solve the larger problem instead because she was too far gone already.

Terk immediately responded to her, which just blew her away.

Stop the talk, focus, and keep your energy to yourself, in case anybody is reading what's going on. I'll only step in when and if I have no other way. Stay calm. We're on it.

She lay here in absolute wonder, shocked that somebody could actually do what he'd just done. Hell, what she'd just done. Again it went back to not really understanding the work they did, but to know that this telepathy was even an option was stunning. More than that, it was, … well, honestly, it was quite scary. But Terk was on her side and for that she was damn glad.

She wanted to see this arrogant asshole die and even spit

in his eye as he took a bullet. She didn't realize how vindictive and mean she'd become, but seeing what was happening to the world around her and how these guys didn't give a shit for human life had changed her. They were so busy trying to take out her and her team, and it had brought out the worst in her, something she wasn't particularly happy about. But she'd deal with that afterward, when the panic wasn't rising through her, knowing that the man she loved and one of the most respected men in her sphere were both riding to her rescue—and certain death.

When the vehicle turned a gentle corner and came to a rolling stop, she realized that they'd reached their destination.

"Now," her kidnapper murmured, "if you're a good girl, I won't have to torture you." He paused. "But, if you'll give me trouble, then you can expect to get beat up some."

Instantly she froze and then nodded quietly.

"Smart. At least, they hired some staff who actually think for themselves," he replied, with a laugh. "Too bad we had to knock y'all off. Because, well, no way we could let anybody live. That's just not part of the job. And anybody who signs up for the type of work you do knows that already."

She wanted to scream in outrage because she hadn't ever thought of something like this being her end, but then neither had Wilson or Mera. Tasha didn't say anything; she just waited until he opened up a door that slid to the side. *I must be in a delivery van.* Then she was grabbed by the feet and dragged halfway across the floor of the vehicle. At the edge she was dropped to her feet. "Now you can stand up. Your hands are tied, but your feet will be free in a sec." She felt a release of pressure around her ankles.

"You give me any guff," he told her, "and I'll pop you

one."

She had no doubt he meant that.

He walked her forward, and she felt the air change as they entered a building.

He muttered, "The damn alarm should have been on, but no worries. I know it takes time and energy to keep that shield up, and nobody has really got energy to spare right now. It makes sense that he would shut it down. I just hope that's all he's done."

She tried to listen to her kidnapper, but she was sending messages as fast as she could to Terk, hoping that somebody was picking them up. Damon was a receiver too, so she immediately started sending him messages. *Stay away. It's a trap. Stay away. It's a trap!*

Terk popped into her mind again. *Stop. You'll cause trouble. Keep your energy to yourself.*

She immediately shut it down. She had a lot to learn, but this would damn well be the last time that they kept this type of shit from her. If Terk could talk to her this way, they could all talk to her this way. Particularly when they were out on jobs. That she was just now finding out about it was absolute bullshit.

Laughter entered her mind, and Damon stepped in. *I'll remember that,* he noted. *Stay quiet and calm. We're coming.*

Like hell, it's a trap.

What you don't know, he told her quietly, *is who is prepared to trap whom here. So please stay calm, behave, and don't get yourself beat up.*

And, with that, she had to stay as quiet as she could, even though it was damn hard. She wanted to turn and kick the crap out of this guy but figured she would probably only get herself beaten up some more.

She probably had already taken a blow or two because her jaw was killing her. The man led her forward, and she just walked at his side calmly. When he came to another door—at least she presumed it was another door—they stopped and he knocked. A muffled response came from the other side. Her kidnapper knocked again, and then he pushed open the door.

"Now we've got both of them," he stated, pushing her in first, as she heard the door close behind them, "and they'll come and do whatever the hell we want now. All we really—" Then he stopped. "Who the hell are you?"

"What do you mean, who the hell am I?" The stranger added, "I'm on your side. I was sent to check up on you."

"We've got it under control. So what the hell are you doing here?" he asked.

Tasha stood frozen, standing still, unsure what to do. What she really wanted to do was drop and roll. The trouble was, with a hood tied on her head, there probably wasn't the space for it, and, for all she knew, it would get her a bullet that wouldn't have been fired otherwise.

"Now raise your hands and don't pull any shit on me," the stranger ordered. "The boss isn't happy with you already, Coop."

"Oh, hell no," her kidnapper muttered. "I'm not dealing with that shit. And here's what I think about that."

A weird buzzing sound filled the air, followed by something popping, and a high-pitched scream.

She impulsively reached up her hands and pulled off her hood. She looked around to see what was probably the newcomer on the ground, completely out cold now. She wasn't even sure he was alive. She gasped. "Did you kill him?"

Her captor turned and looked at her with an ugly expression, his fist still clenched. "You took your blindfold off," he growled. "You'll pay for that."

Yep, she recognized that voice. *Her kidnapper. The man called Coop.* She stared at him in shock. "Did you just kill him?"

"I had to. We really can't leave anybody alive anymore, and that includes you." He lunged toward her, the blow coming out of the blue.

She cried out in agony, dropping to her knees. She watched in surprise when the guy on the floor sat up, gun in hand, and he fired several shots at Coop.

Coop cried out, "No, not even bullets will stop me."

But something else was happening. She watched in shock and horror as some weird—telepathic?—fight was going on. Coop had his eyes closed, like Terk does at times, but Coop faced the stranger, who had been disarmed and taken down to the floor again ... somehow.

Coop had drawn his weapon, had it in his hand, and she tried to get it away from him. But he tossed her to the ground again, even as Damon raced toward them. Coop raised his gun and fired once.

Seeing Damon take a shot high in the chest, Tasha immediately jumped on Coop. She grabbed his gun arm, twisting it against his body, and she pulled the trigger again and again and again. He collapsed to the floor beside her, just as two more men burst in. She looked at Terk and a man who clearly had to be his brother. She shook her head. "Jesus Christ, you are undeniably twins."

Terk looked at her quickly, then raced to Damon. Merk came to her, studied the dead guy closest to her. "He's dead."

"Coop is dead? Are you certain?" she asked. "Honest to

God, we need to put ten bullets in his brain just to make sure because he dropped that other man just by standing here, only using his mind." Merk stared at her in shock, and she nodded quietly. "You have no idea how crazy this is!"

She turned to Damon, who was struggling on the other side of the room. She raced over and dropped to her knees. "Jesus, Damon. No! No!"

The bullet wound was high, but it didn't look very good. The hole was pulsing blood, and Merk immediately went into first aid action.

She looked over at Terk, worried. "We've got to do something."

"I'm sorry," he said, "but I have to do this."

She looked at him in shock. "What do you mean?"

He smiled. "Hopefully it won't feel too bad."

With that, he reached over and grabbed her hand. And suddenly she was caught up in a kaleidoscope of emotions, nightmarish colors, and sounds, almost like being in a whirlpool, while screaming to get out. Maybe a tornado was a better description. And suddenly she reached a calm spot.

She looked to see Terk inside a weird space. He talked to her, but his voice was like an echo.

He told her, "Talk to Damon. Tell him that you love him. Tell him that he needs to come back to you."

She stared at him in shock. "Is he dead?"

"He's on the cusp," Terk replied. "You'll lose him now, but maybe, if we pull together, we might help him."

She dropped to her knees, her hands cupping Damon's face, as she whispered against his lips, "Please, Damon, come back. Come back to me. We never even had a chance together. Please, dear God, come back."

Just when she thought there was absolutely no hope, a

voice whispered through her mind.

He got you with that, did he?

With what? she cried out to Damon, tears in her eyes.

Now we're connected in a way that you have no idea about.

I don't care, as long as we're connected.

But, if I die, you die.

What? she asked, feeling confused, then she got crafty. *That just means you have to fight because otherwise you're killing me.*

He groaned at that. *It hurts.*

I know, she whispered. *I know, but please fight.* She looked over to see Terk standing there, energy flowing around in this weird cosmic tunnel, flowing into Damon and out again. "Use my energy if you need to," she cried out.

"I already am," he murmured. "Just let me finish."

And, with that, she had to sit back and watch, as a healthier color slowly returned to Damon's face.

She looked down at the chest wound and shuddered. Her hand went to his chest but almost went through it. And she realized that, whatever form she was in, it wasn't physical. It was like she had stepped out of her own body, but then she realized she hadn't stepped out—she'd been pulled out by Terk.

She watched Merk's face, seeing the disbelief there, as he realized how quickly Damon was improving.

With the weird energy all around the room, Merk stared at his brother, studying his face. "Terk, I love you, man. But you are one damn scary dude."

She gently stroked Damon's face, feeling him jerk back in surprise. She smiled. "But he's a hell of a good guy," she told Merk. "And right now he's saving Damon."

And just like that she felt a weird pull inside her, and she was snapped back into her body. She rocked in place, as she landed. She opened her eyes, stared around her, and whispered, "I don't know what the hell just happened or how you even did that," she noted, "but, if you ever do that again, Terk, I just might kill you myself."

Terk laughed. "Not if it does the job," he murmured, and he dropped beside Damon.

Reaching up, Tasha cupped Damon's cheek and whispered, "Open your eyes, Damon. Please? Are you there?"

He opened his eyes, those huge steely gray eyes that were now the softest of colors. He looked over at her, and he smiled. "Hey, welcome home." He'd reached up a hand and placed it over her heart.

She immediately covered his hands with her own, pulling them up to her lips, where she kissed them. "You are now officially out of action."

He shook his head. "Oh, hell no."

"Yes, you are. Until you get this chest wound fixed and are rested up, you're not going back out on a job."

He looked over at Terk. "We're too shorthanded for that."

Terk shook his head. "She's right. You're too injured."

"We need somebody to help."

And there beside them, speaking in a raspy voice, was another male. She looked over to see Wade sit up in bed.

He smiled at her. "Welcome to the team."

She reached out a hand, and he grasped it, and she felt the energy flowing from Terk through her to Wade.

"Dear God." They hugged gently. "Are you okay?"

"I am now." Wade stretched, rotated his neck and his body a bit. "I'm not sure how long I've been out, and it'll probably take me a couple days to really snap back, but, man, oh man, am I glad to be out of that fugue." He looked down at Damon. "And you look like shit, buddy."

Damon gave him a lopsided grin. "Yeah, but I got the girl."

Wade looked at her, then to Damon. "Hell, I told you to take care of that years ago."

"I know. I should have," Damon agreed. "But now she has given me a reason to live again, so I'll take it."

Wade nodded at Merk, then took in Terk, glancing back again to Merk. "Good Lord."

Merk smiled. "I know. We really are twins."

The two looked so much alike.

Merk reached out a hand to his brother. They gripped each other's hands for a long moment, and Merk asked, "Do you guys need us to handle this?"

They looked at the two dead bodies, and Wade paled. "Jesus. That's Paul. I could feel him, sense him here, but…"

Terk crouch down beside him. "I'm sorry. He was part of all this."

Wade pinched his lips. "He was always against me. Hated me really. I can't say I'm surprised, but I am… sorry." He crouched down beside his brother, laid a hand on his shoulder and closed his eyes.

Straightening, Terk replied to Merk, "Yeah, if you could handle that, it'd be great. None of us are supposed to be alive. Remember?"

"I'll arrange for it," Merk replied, "and I'll get a panel van or something in here and get you guys moved out discreetly. These two won't do much for quite a while."

"I'll take Wade and Damon back to our headquarters," she stated, "and we'll keep them there with us." Then she frowned. "No, we shouldn't have Damon anywhere near that stuff. He'll want to work."

"No," Terk added, "short of you staying with Damon, *you* are needed at work."

She looked over at Terk. "Solution?"

"We have a new base," he noted, "so we'll get you and Damon to move to a hotel for now, and, with help from Wade and Merk, we'll move the entire operation there. Tasha, you'll be happy to hear it has actual bedrooms."

"Perfect," Damon agreed. As they headed off to make arrangements, he called out, "And just one room for us, okay? Don't piss me off by putting her in her own."

"Why is that?" she asked. "Even if we wanted to be together, I could just come over to your room."

He shook his head. "Nope," he argued. "I'm pretty sure this guy probably got off a couple messages, so you will now be target number one."

She shook her head. "That won't matter. If he had any idea that Wade is alive, Wade would be target number one."

Damon frowned, nodded. "Damn. Okay, fine. You can have your own bedroom then."

"Too bad," she said. "I don't want one."

And, with that, she leaned over and kissed him.

CHAPTER 15

I T TOOK FOUR days. Four long days of moving computer equipment and other items. Tasha and Damon were in a hotel room during that transition period and were then moved to the new base at the outskirts of Manchester, England. They did have one shared bedroom, with a very large king-size bed, on which she was even now studying the sleeping man beside her. She hadn't slept very much in the last few days, and, by the time she finished her night's ablutions, she crawled into bed, but she was still too tired to sleep.

He wrapped an arm around her and pulled her close.

"It still feels so weird," she noted. "Not only just the two of us together now but to think that, for the moment, we're safe."

"Don't ever think that."

She winced. "Okay, fine. Not *safe*-safe. But it just feels like, I don't know. I guess I'm still just uptight and unnerved about the whole thing."

"As much as I hate to say it, that's actually a good thing. We do have to be wary, and we always have to be alert, no matter what."

"I get it." She rolled over and smiled at him. "I still can't believe you're alive after that."

"I don't deserve to be, but it's thanks to you that I am."

"I don't know that it's so much thanks to me but definitely thanks to Terk."

"Both," he agreed. "I'm good at some things, but Terk has been pushing the boundaries so far and so fast that we've gotten really worried about him. But he's done it so he could teach us. It wasn't just him with these abilities," he murmured. "But it's been scary watching him go down that pathway, pushing himself to the point where you wonder how much of this is even normal anymore."

"None of it's normal," she noted quietly, "but I have seen enough now that I will never take for granted even the simplest things in life anymore."

"Good," he replied, "that's one good thing then."

She added, "Now that Wade is up and alive, I need to backtrack Coop, my kidnapper, and that other guy he killed, Paul – Wade's brother, and see where we go from here."

"Yes, and I'll get back on my feet and do something about that soon, like maybe tomorrow."

"Like hell," she said. "I might bring you a laptop or something to keep you happy, but you're not leaving this bed until the doctor okays it."

"And who the hell thought it was a good idea to bring in a doctor on this anyway?" he muttered.

"I did," she snapped. "Anything to keep you safe."

He rolled his eyes at that. "I was healing just fine, you know?"

"You were healing, yes, but you're still not healthy. Besides, it was Merk's connection, and he, well, Merk seems to have connections all over the place."

Damon laughed. "So do we. What did he say, by the way?"

"That you're to stay in bed for the next couple weeks."

"No way in hell I'm doing that," he barked. "Those kinds of lies won't get you anywhere."

She smiled, then leaned over and added, "Okay, fine. He said to stay in bed for a week, and then you can slowly start to resume some easy activity."

He reached up, grabbed her, and pulled her close. "You know that my chest is doing much better. I can get up. I can stretch, and I'm even doing some of those exercises."

"Not so fast," she said.

"Well, how about other exercises?" He waggled his eyes.

"Hell no," she murmured. "That's definitely out."

"It's *never* definitely out," he snapped in a light tone as he leaned over and kissed her. "I've wanted this for a very long time, you know?"

"In that case you can wait for a little bit longer."

He smiled. "It's really good for stress relief."

"Yeah, like I'll get sucked into that," she argued, but she was smiling.

"It is good to see you feeling so happy."

"Hey, nothing like having all that energy flow through me. It's a miracle in a way. But it was pretty scary."

He kissed her gently and then kissed her again. Before she knew it, she was flat on her back, and he was lying gently at her side. And his hands were underneath her nightie.

"Good God." She twisted beneath him. "You are bloody dangerous."

"I am when I'm focused," he muttered, "and you know how focused I can be."

She glared at him. "It's still a no."

"What if I made it a *maybe?*"

She burst out laughing. "How are there *maybes* in this world?"

"There are tons of maybes," he noted. "See? Like maybe you want me to kiss you like this," he murmured, gently kissing first her lips, then her cheeks, and then her temples. "And maybe you want me to do a little more, like kiss you down here." He slid the lacey gown up to her collarbone, where he kissed just underneath and all the way down to her breastbone.

She arched beneath him. "It's really not a good idea."

"And I guarantee you," he murmured, as he kissed her some more, then sliding his tongue over her plump breast, taking her nipple deep into his mouth, "this is exactly what the doctor ordered."

She was beyond talking when he suckled her other breast. "Be careful of your chest," she mumbled in amazement.

"I'm doing better."

"Yeah, but you can't be that much better."

"Oh, you might be surprised." And he slid his fingers down to the apex of her thighs.

She shuddered out a gasp. "My God."

"I'll be gentle," he murmured.

At that, she burst out laughing, only to have her laughs turned to groans, as he slid into the soft, moist folds at the heart of her. "Gentle? You'll be gentle with me?" she teased. "You should be gentle with yourself."

"I promise, slow and steady. Just like pushups."

She groaned at that analogy. "You seriously won't—" And then he was right there. She opened her thighs wider, as he slid all the way home. She shuddered at the feel of him. "My God," she whispered. "Why the hell did we wait all these years?"

"Because I'm a fool." He held one of her hands gently to

his chest.

"If you hurt yourself …" she warned.

"Yeah, you'll do what?" he asked, gently teasing her lips with his own.

"I might just force you to go to bed and to stay there for a little longer," she whispered. "And, if you're a really bad boy, I might just crawl in there with you."

"Where the hell is the incentive to be good?" he asked her in amazement.

She smiled. "Because, if you'd be good, I might keep you in bed for the next month, just to make sure that you're healing properly."

He lowered his head. "You can take me to bed any damn time you want to. But I would like a little more than just having you in my bed. Given a choice, I'd like to keep you in my heart, which, as you well know, is exactly where you belong."

She slid her arms around his neck and whispered, "Done. That's a deal I can get behind."

When he lowered his head and started to move, she thought she'd died and gone to heaven. Her body vibrated at an odd rate only to sudden calm, as if in an eye of a storm. She opened her eyes to see the two of them enwrapped in a weird bubble. "Energy?" she asked in a barest whisper.

"Love."

And damn if the vibration didn't speed up, but now it was smoother, more intense, and somehow she knew it was both their energies joined, … as one. When she exploded minutes later, hearing him join her on the cusp of an orgasm, she knew that her life, even though it had been hellish for a few weeks, was about to get a whole lot better.

By the time he collapsed beside her, she checked him

over and asked, "Are you hurt?"

"Never," he breathed. "Personally I think that's a hell of a good way to exercise my chest muscles. We should do it again soon." He closed his eyes and dropped into a deep sleep.

She lay snuggled up tightly against him, wondering how beautiful life would get for them as a couple. Yeah, she was well aware of a lot of shitty aspects to this situation right now, but, with him at her side, she figured she'd handle anything that came her way.

EPILOGUE

WADE SIMCO WANDERED the small space. "Why are we in here? The place is empty." He turned to look at Terk.

"We're here," Terk replied, "because this concrete room is reinforced with steel. We need to build a tunnel to get out through but to also stop anybody from coming in."

"You really think it's that Iranian group we hunted down who's attacking us? But we thought we got them all?"

Terk nodded. "Like they thought they got all of us."

Wade shook his head. "I don't see how anybody could have survived our attack. Didn't you have Tasha checking that angle?"

"She's still working on it. Will take some time. But the Iranian group could have been training a shadow crew for all we knew. And I don't know anybody else with the same skills," he stated. "Didn't your brother train over there?" At Wade's silent nod, Terk added, "So, considering that, maybe Iran is our best option."

"I got it," Wade said, "but damn."

"I know. I know," Terk agreed. "And we need more people. Merk is bringing in somebody else to help with communication."

"What about Tasha?" Wade asked.

"Oh, we definitely need her, but we also need somebody

else to help Tasha and us. According to Merk, this person is really good."

"Have you ever worked with him before?"

"*Her*. No, I haven't, but I trust my brother. It's somebody he has known for a long time, although he did say that she had worked for the team but more as a freelancer."

"That sounds dodgy."

"Well, in my experience, hackers tend to be that way," he noted.

"Yeah, that's true enough. Look at Tasha," he murmured. "I can't believe she and Damon finally got together. I've been bugging him about that since she first joined us."

"Yes," Terk agreed, "I think we all have. But at least he's finally getting it right."

"I'm happy for him," Wade muttered.

"So am I. They'll be good together," he agreed.

"And now that we have them together, the problem is, how to keep them safe."

"Right," Terk nodded, "and that's why we're bringing in another operative."

"Got it," Wade replied.

Terk cocked his head. "As matter of fact, they should be here any moment."

"Great. Do I know her?"

"I don't think so," Terk said, "but I could be wrong." He looked over at Wade and asked, "How are you handling your brother and all?"

"It's a sad thing," he replied, "but I always figured my brother would end up dead on a job one day. Just some people always want to be on the wrong side of life. They don't give a shit about anything but themselves, and that was my brother. I loved him. I really did. But, in the end, I couldn't save him."

"And that's good enough for me," Terk said. "Nothing's easy about family, particularly if you're on the wrong side of things when it comes down to the end."

"No, not easy at all. He's gone, and—unfortunately or maybe not—maybe I'm grateful that my mom is also gone, so she didn't see what happened and didn't have to deal with the fact that we don't have a body to bury," he murmured.

"No, and I'm sorry if that's an issue."

"It isn't. My brother probably would have preferred this in a way. As sad as it seems, I think he would like to be a ghost in the world."

Just then Terk straightened. "We have company." He walked out into the other room as a *click* came at the door, and Merk walked in. But Terk's gaze was drawn to the woman at his brother's side and how her energy zinged right to Wade. Terk was surprised because he hadn't seen a foreshadowing of that happening at all.

Merk smiled. "And this is Sophia."

She stepped forward, looked at the men in front of her, then frowned when she saw Wade. "*You*, I know," she snapped.

He stared at her, as a grin crossed his face. "Well now, isn't that fun." He looked over at Terk. "We knew each other a while back."

Terk looked at him. "Knew?"

He shrugged. "Knew in the biblical sense. Not the long-term sense."

The woman snorted. "I think the last thing out of your mouth was, 'See you later.'"

"Sure, and here I am. It's later."

"Are you?" she asked, and she glared at him. "You were

supposed to come for dinner that night."

"And then I got called to a job," Wade said easily. He looked at Terk. "She's your new hire?"

Terk turned to his brother. Merk nodded. "She's hell-bent for whatever sounds like technology."

Wade nodded. "And that's how we hooked up. We were at a seminar."

"Yeah, they didn't know anything there." She shook her head.

"Which is how we ended up together that night," he explained easily. "Because both of us had the same opinion."

Just then another door opened, and Damon came out, walking very slowly, Tasha at his side.

Tasha took one look and said, "Sophia?"

Sophia's face lit up, and she came running. The two women hugged each other, and Sophia whispered, "Oh my God, there you are. All the others are talking about what you did."

"I know. I'm very lucky that I survived," Tasha replied. "We're hunting those who tried to take us out."

Sophia looked at Merk and asked, "Is this true?"

Merk nodded. "Terk's team here was the target. He and Damon have been trying to piece things together. Wade was one of the casualties. He's only barely back. In fact, he woke up from a coma just a few days ago."

She turned her concerned gaze to Wade.

He shrugged. "I'm fine."

She nodded. "Good, then I can kick your ass later."

He grinned and said, "You can try."

"Count on it," she snapped, "and I'll win too." She walked over to Terk, reached out a hand, and, when he placed his in hers, she studied Terk for a long moment.

Everybody in the room could see the energy rise up ever-so-slightly. "Fine." She nodded. "I'm in."

"We can't have you come in and then walk out," he murmured quietly. "This has to be a 100 percent commitment. We have to know that we can trust you and that you'll have our backs."

She looked at Terk and frowned. "It's only because you don't know me that I'll allow you to say that. After this moment, you don't ever get to misjudge me again. When I say, *I'm in*, then I'm in. Done deal." She looked over at Wade, frowned at him. "You and I, however, still have a score to settle."

He nodded. "Maybe. I'm looking forward to it. And welcome to the team."

She smiled, looked around at Tasha. "Now I feel better. This is a family I do know, and I'm more than happy to help out."

And, with that, she looked at the equipment set up in the main outer room and asked, "So, where do I start?"

This concludes Book 1 of Terkel's Team: Damon's Deal.
Read about Wade's War: Terkel's Team, Book 2

Terkel's Team: Wade's War (Book #2)

Welcome to a brand-new series from *USA Today* best-selling author Dale Mayer, where dark-ops SEALs have special senses and skills, needed to solve intrigue, betrayal, and … murder. A series with all the elements you've come to love, plus so much more, … including psychics!

Sophia met Wade a few years back, and the last she heard from him was he'd be back to take her out to dinner—and never saw him again. Having spent several years in the meantime working with Merk and his team in Texas, when Terk called for her help, Sophia jumped at the opportunity to go. Even if Wade didn't get it, she knew a connection worth trying for when she felt it.

Wade is weak, helpless, his abilities damaged, after the attack on Terk's team. Seeing Sophia, the woman he fell in love with at first sight, is a sock to his gut. His defenses are already down, and he knows it will be impossible to keep her at arm's length a second time.

Wade must bring her closer, protect her, especially after

their team was shattered from the initial attack, and subsequent attacks haven't eased—not with the world slowly realizing that not just Terk survived the attack but so did a few of his team …

Find Book 2 here!

To find out more visit Dale Mayer's website.

https://geni.us/DMTTWadeUniversal

Magnus: Shadow Recon (Book #1)

Deep in the permafrost of the Arctic, a joint task force, comprised of over one dozen countries, comes together to level up their winter skills. A mix of personalities, nationalities, and egos bring out the best—and the worst—as these globally elite men and women work and play together. They rub elbows with hardy locals and a group of scientists gathered close by …

One fatality is almost expected with this training. A second is tough but not a surprise. However, when a third goes missing? It's hard to not be suspicious. When the missing man is connected to one of the elite Maverick team members and is a special friend of Lieutenant Commander Mason Callister? All hell breaks loose …

L IEUTENANT COMMANDER MASON Callister walked into the private office and stood in front of retired Navy Commander Doran Magellan.

"Mason, good to see you."

Yet the dry tone of voice, and the scowl pinching the silver-haired man, all belied his words. Mason had known Doran for over a decade, and their friendship had only grown over time.

Mason waited, as he watched the other man try to work the new tech phone system on his desk. With his hand circling the air above the black box, he appeared to hit buttons randomly.

Mason held back his amusement but to no avail.

"Why can't a phone be a phone anymore?" the commander snapped, as his glare shifted from Mason to the box and back.

Asking the commander if he needed help wouldn't make the older man feel any better, but sitting here and watching as he indiscriminately punched buttons was a struggle. "Is Helen away?" Mason asked.

"Yes, damn it. She's at lunch, and I need her to be at lunch." The commander's piercing gaze pinned Mason in place. "No one is to know you're here."

Solemn, Mason nodded. "Understood."

"Doran? Is that you?" A crotchety voice slammed into the room through the phone's speakers. "Get away from that damn phone. You keep clicking buttons in my ear. Get

Helen in there to do this."

"No, she can't be here for this."

Silence came first, then a huge groan. "Damn it. Then you should have connected me last, so I don't have to sit here and listen to you fumbling around."

"Go pour yourself a damn drink then," Doran barked. "I'm working on the others."

A snort was his only response.

Mason bit the inside of his lip, as he really tried to hold back his grin. The retired commander had been hell on wheels while on active duty, and, even now, the retired part of his life seemed to be more of a euphemism than anything.

"Damn things …"

Mason looked around the dark mahogany office and the walls filled with photos, awards, medals. A life of purpose, accomplishment. And all of that had only piqued his interest during the initial call he'd received, telling him to be here at this time.

"Ah, got it."

Mason's eyebrows barely twitched, as the commander gave him a feral grin. "I'd rather lead a warship into battle than deal with some of today's technology."

As he was one of only a few commanders who'd been in a position to do such a thing, it said much about his capabilities.

And much about current technology.

The commander leaned back in his massive chair and motioned to the cart beside Mason. "Pour three cups."

Interesting. Mason walked a couple steps across the rich tapestry-style carpet and lifted the silver service to pour coffee into three very down-to-earth-looking mugs.

"Black for me."

Mason picked up two cups and walked one over to Doran.

"Thanks." He leaned forward and snapped into the phone, "Everyone here?"

Multiple voices responded.

Curiouser and curiouser. Mason recognized several of the voices. Other relics of an era gone by. Although not a one would like to hear that, and, in good faith, it wasn't fair. Mason had thought each of these men were retired, had relinquished power. Yet, as he studied Doran in front of him, Mason had to wonder if any of them actually had passed the baton or if they'd only slid into the shadows. Was this planned with the government's authority? Or were these retirees a shadow group to the government?

The tangible sense of power and control oozed from Doran's words, tone, stature—his very pores. This man might be heading into his sunset years—based on a simple calculation of chronological years spent on the planet—but he was a long way from being out of the action.

"Mason …" Doran began.

"Sir?"

"We've got a problem."

Mason narrowed his gaze and waited.

Doran's glare was hard, steely hard, with an icy glint. "Do you know the Mavericks?"

Mason's eyebrows shot up. The black ops division was one of those well-kept secrets, so, therefore, everyone knew about it. He gave a decisive nod. "I do."

"And you're involved in the logistics behind the ICE training program in the Arctic, are you not?"

"I am." Now where was the commander going with this?

"Do you know another SEAL by the name of Mountain

Rode? He's been working for the black ops Mavericks." At his own words, the commander shook his head. "What the hell was his mother thinking when she gave him that moniker?"

"She wasn't thinking anything," said the man with a hard voice from behind Mason.

He stiffened slightly, then relaxed as he recognized that voice too.

"She died giving birth to me. And my full legal name is Mountain Bear Rode. It was my father's doing."

The commander glared at the new arrival. "Did I say you could come in?"

"Yes." Mountain's voice was firm, yet a definitive note of affection filled his tone.

That emotion told Mason so much.

The commander harrumphed, then cleared his throat. "Mason, we're picking up a significant amount of chatter over that ICE training. Most of it good. Some of it the usual caterwauling we've come to expect every time we participate in a joint training mission. This one is set to run for six months, then to reassess."

Mason already knew this. But he waited for the commander to get around to why Mason was here, and, more important, what any of this had to do with the mountain of a man who now towered beside him.

The commander shifted his gaze to Mountain, but he remained silent.

Mason noted Mountain was not only physically big but damn imposing and severely pissed, seemingly barely holding back the forces within. His body language seemed to yell, *And the world will fix this, or I'll find the reason why.*

For a moment Mason felt sorry for the world.

Finally a voice spoke through the phone. "Mason, this is Alpha here. I run the Mavericks. We've got a problem with that ICE training center. Mountain, tell him."

Mason shifted to include Mountain in his field of vision. Mason wished the other men on the conference call were in the room too. It was one thing to deal with men you knew and could take the measure of; it was another when they were silent shadows in the background.

"My brother is one of the men who reported for the Artic training three weeks ago."

"Tergan Rode?" Mason confirmed. "I'm the one who arranged for him to go up there. He's a great kid."

A glimmer of a smile cracked Mountain's stony features. He nodded. "Indeed. A bright light in my often dark world. He's a dozen years younger than me, just passed his BUD/s training this spring, and raring to go. Until his raring to go then got up and went."

Oh, shit. Mason's gaze zinged to the commander, who had kicked up his feet to rest atop the big desk. Stocking feet. With Mickey Mouse images dancing on them. Sidetracked, Mason struggled to pull his attention back to Mountain. "Meaning?"

"He's disappeared." Mountain let out a harsh breath, as if just saying that out loud, and maybe to the right people, could allow him to relax—at least a little.

The commander spoke up. "We need your help, Mason. You're uniquely qualified for this problem."

It didn't sound like he was qualified in any way for anything he'd heard so far. "Clarify." His spoken word was simplicity itself, but the tone behind it said he wanted the cards on the table … now.

Mountain spoke up. "He's the third incident."

Mason's gaze narrowed, as the reports from the training

camp rolled through his mind. "One was Russian. One was from the German SEAL team. Both were deemed accidental deaths."

"No, they weren't."

There it was. The root of the problem in black-and-white. He studied Mountain, aiming for neutrality. "Do you have evidence?"

"My brother did."

"Ah, hell."

Mountain gave a clipped nod. "I'm going to find him."

"Of that I have no doubt," Mason said quietly. "Do you have a copy of the evidence he collected?"

"I have some of it." Mountain held out a USB key. "This is your copy. Top secret."

"We don't have to remind you, Mason, that lives are at stake," Doran added. "Nor do we need another international incident. Consider also that a group of scientists, studying global warming, is close by, and not too far away is a village home to a few hardy locals."

Mason accepted the key, turned to the commander, and asked, "Do we know if this is internal or enemy warfare?"

"We don't know at this point," Alpha replied through the phone. "Mountain will lead Shadow Recon. His mission is twofold. One, find out what's behind these so-called accidents and put a stop to it by any means necessary. Two, locate his brother, hopefully alive."

"And where do I come in?" Mason asked.

"We want you to pull together a special team. The members of Shadow Recon will report to both you and Mountain, just in case."

That was clear enough.

"You'll stay stateside but in constant communication with Mountain—with the caveat that, if necessary, you're on the next flight out.”

“What about bringing in other members from the Mavericks?” Mason suggested.

Alpha took this question too, his response coming through via Speakerphone. “We don’t have the numbers. The budget for our division has been cut. So we called the commander to pull some strings.”

That was Doran’s cue to explain further. “Mountain has fought hard to get me on board with this plan, and I’m here now. The navy has a special budget for Shadow Recon and will take care of Mountain and you, Mason, and the team you provide.”

“Skills needed?”

“Everything,” Mountain said, his voice harsh. “But the biggest is these men need to operate in the shadows, mostly alone, without a team beside them. Too many new arrivals will alert the enemy. If we make any changes to the training program, it will raise alarms. We’ll move the men in one or two at a time on the same rotation that the trainees are running right now.”

“And when we get to the bottom of this?” Mason looked from the commander back to Mountain.

“Then the training can resume as usual,” Doran stated.

Mason immediately churned through the names already popping up in his mind. How much could he tell his men? Obviously not much. Hell, he didn’t know much himself. How much time did he have? “Timeline?”

The commander’s final word told him of the urgency.

“Yesterday.”

Find Magnus here!

To find out more visit Dale Mayer’s website.

https://geni.us/DMSRMagnusUniversal

Author's Note

Thank you for reading Damon's Deal: Terkel's Team, Book 1! If you enjoyed the book, please take a moment and leave a short review.

Dear reader,

I love to hear from readers, and you can contact me at my website: www.dalemayer.com or at my Facebook author page. To be informed of new releases and special offers, sign up for my newsletter or follow me on BookBub. And if you are interested in joining Dale Mayer's Reader Group, here is the Facebook sign up page.
http://geni.us/DaleMayerFBGroup

Cheers,
Dale Mayer

Get THREE Free Books Now!

Have you met the SEALS of Honor?

SEALs of Honor Books 1, 2, and 3. Follow the stories of brave, badass warriors who serve their country with honor and love their women to the limits of life and death.

Read Mason, Hawk, and Dane right now for FREE.

Go here and tell me where to send them!
https://dalemayer.com/masonfree

About the Author

Dale Mayer is a *USA Today* best-selling author, best known for her SEALs military romances, her Psychic Visions series, and her Lovely Lethal Garden cozy series. Her contemporary romances are raw and full of passion and emotion (Broken But … Mending, Hathaway House series). Her thrillers will keep you guessing (Kate Morgan, By Death series), and her romantic comedies will keep you giggling (*It's a Dog's Life*, a stand-alone novella; and the Broken Protocols series, starring Charming Marvin, the cat).

Dale honors the stories that come to her—and some of them are crazy, break all the rules and cross multiple genres!

To go with her fiction, she also writes nonfiction in many different fields, with books available on résumé writing, companion gardening, and the US mortgage system. All her books are available in print and ebook format.

Connect with Dale Mayer Online

Dale's Website – www.dalemayer.com
Twitter – @DaleMayer
Facebook Page – geni.us/DaleMayerFBFanPage
Facebook Group – geni.us/DaleMayerFBGroup
BookBub – geni.us/DaleMayerBookbub
Instagram – geni.us/DaleMayerInstagram
Goodreads – geni.us/DaleMayerGoodreads
Newsletter – geni.us/DaleNews

Also by Dale Mayer

Published Adult Books:

Bullard's Battle
Ryland's Reach, Book 1
Cain's Cross, Book 2
Eton's Escape, Book 3
Garret's Gambit, Book 4
Kano's Keep, Book 5
Fallon's Flaw, Book 6
Quinn's Quest, Book 7
Bullard's Beauty, Book 8
Bullard's Best, Book 9

Terkel's Team
Damon's Deal, Book 1
Wade's War, Book 2
Gage's Goal, Book 3
Calum's Contact, Book 4

Kate Morgan
Simon Says… Hide, Book 1
Simon Says… Jump, Book 2
Simon Says… Ride, Book 3
Simon Says… Scream, Book 4

Hathaway House

Aaron, Book 1
Brock, Book 2
Cole, Book 3
Denton, Book 4
Elliot, Book 5
Finn, Book 6
Gregory, Book 7
Heath, Book 8
Iain, Book 9
Jaden, Book 10
Keith, Book 11
Lance, Book 12
Melissa, Book 13
Nash, Book 14
Owen, Book 15
Percy, Book 16
Hathaway House, Books 1–3
Hathaway House, Books 4–6
Hathaway House, Books 7–9

The K9 Files

Ethan, Book 1
Pierce, Book 2
Zane, Book 3
Blaze, Book 4
Lucas, Book 5
Parker, Book 6
Carter, Book 7
Weston, Book 8
Greyson, Book 9
Rowan, Book 10

Caleb, Book 11
Kurt, Book 12
Tucker, Book 13
Harley, Book 14
Kyron, Book 15
Jenner, Book 16
The K9 Files, Books 1–2
The K9 Files, Books 3–4
The K9 Files, Books 5–6
The K9 Files, Books 7–8
The K9 Files, Books 9–10
The K9 Files, Books 11–12

Lovely Lethal Gardens

Arsenic in the Azaleas, Book 1
Bones in the Begonias, Book 2
Corpse in the Carnations, Book 3
Daggers in the Dahlias, Book 4
Evidence in the Echinacea, Book 5
Footprints in the Ferns, Book 6
Gun in the Gardenias, Book 7
Handcuffs in the Heather, Book 8
Ice Pick in the Ivy, Book 9
Jewels in the Juniper, Book 10
Killer in the Kiwis, Book 11
Lifeless in the Lilies, Book 12
Murder in the Marigolds, Book 13
Nabbed in the Nasturtiums, Book 14
Offed in the Orchids, Book 15
Poison in the Pansies, Book 16
Quarry in the Quince, Book 17
Lovely Lethal Gardens, Books 1–2

Lovely Lethal Gardens, Books 3–4
Lovely Lethal Gardens, Books 5–6
Lovely Lethal Gardens, Books 7–8
Lovely Lethal Gardens, Books 9–10

Psychic Vision Series

Tuesday's Child
Hide 'n Go Seek
Maddy's Floor
Garden of Sorrow
Knock Knock…
Rare Find
Eyes to the Soul
Now You See Her
Shattered
Into the Abyss
Seeds of Malice
Eye of the Falcon
Itsy-Bitsy Spider
Unmasked
Deep Beneath
From the Ashes
Stroke of Death
Ice Maiden
Snap, Crackle…
What If…
Talking Bones
Psychic Visions Books 1–3
Psychic Visions Books 4–6
Psychic Visions Books 7–9

By Death Series
Touched by Death
Haunted by Death
Chilled by Death
By Death Books 1–3

Broken Protocols – Romantic Comedy Series
Cat's Meow
Cat's Pajamas
Cat's Cradle
Cat's Claus
Broken Protocols 1-4

Broken and... Mending
Skin
Scars
Scales (of Justice)
Broken but... Mending 1-3

Glory
Genesis
Tori
Celeste
Glory Trilogy

Biker Blues
Morgan: Biker Blues, Volume 1
Cash: Biker Blues, Volume 2

SEALs of Honor
Mason: SEALs of Honor, Book 1
Hawk: SEALs of Honor, Book 2

SEALs of Honor, Books 20–22
SEALs of Honor, Books 23–25

Heroes for Hire

Levi's Legend: Heroes for Hire, Book 1
Stone's Surrender: Heroes for Hire, Book 2
Merk's Mistake: Heroes for Hire, Book 3
Rhodes's Reward: Heroes for Hire, Book 4
Flynn's Firecracker: Heroes for Hire, Book 5
Logan's Light: Heroes for Hire, Book 6
Harrison's Heart: Heroes for Hire, Book 7
Saul's Sweetheart: Heroes for Hire, Book 8
Dakota's Delight: Heroes for Hire, Book 9
Tyson's Treasure: Heroes for Hire, Book 10
Jace's Jewel: Heroes for Hire, Book 11
Rory's Rose: Heroes for Hire, Book 12
Brandon's Bliss: Heroes for Hire, Book 13
Liam's Lily: Heroes for Hire, Book 14
North's Nikki: Heroes for Hire, Book 15
Anders's Angel: Heroes for Hire, Book 16
Reyes's Raina: Heroes for Hire, Book 17
Dezi's Diamond: Heroes for Hire, Book 18
Vince's Vixen: Heroes for Hire, Book 19
Ice's Icing: Heroes for Hire, Book 20
Johan's Joy: Heroes for Hire, Book 21
Galen's Gemma: Heroes for Hire, Book 22
Zack's Zest: Heroes for Hire, Book 23
Bonaparte's Belle: Heroes for Hire, Book 24
Noah's Nemesis: Heroes for Hire, Book 25
Tomas's Trials: Heroes for Hire, Book 26
Heroes for Hire, Books 1–3
Heroes for Hire, Books 4–6

Heroes for Hire, Books 7–9
Heroes for Hire, Books 10–12
Heroes for Hire, Books 13–15
Heroes for Hire, Books 16–18
Heroes for Hire, Books 19–21
Heroes for Hire, Books 22–24

SEALs of Steel

Badger: SEALs of Steel, Book 1
Erick: SEALs of Steel, Book 2
Cade: SEALs of Steel, Book 3
Talon: SEALs of Steel, Book 4
Laszlo: SEALs of Steel, Book 5
Geir: SEALs of Steel, Book 6
Jager: SEALs of Steel, Book 7
The Final Reveal: SEALs of Steel, Book 8
SEALs of Steel, Books 1–4
SEALs of Steel, Books 5–8
SEALs of Steel, Books 1–8

The Mavericks

Kerrick, Book 1
Griffin, Book 2
Jax, Book 3
Beau, Book 4
Asher, Book 5
Ryker, Book 6
Miles, Book 7
Nico, Book 8
Keane, Book 9
Lennox, Book 10
Gavin, Book 11

Shane, Book 12
Diesel, Book 13
Jerricho, Book 14
Killian, Book 15
Hatch, Book 16
Corbin, Book 17
The Mavericks, Books 1–2
The Mavericks, Books 3–4
The Mavericks, Books 5–6
The Mavericks, Books 7–8
The Mavericks, Books 9–10
The Mavericks, Books 11–12

Collections

Dare to Be You…
Dare to Love…
Dare to be Strong…
RomanceX3

Standalone Novellas

It's a Dog's Life
Riana's Revenge
Second Chances

Published Young Adult Books:

Family Blood Ties Series

Vampire in Denial
Vampire in Distress
Vampire in Design
Vampire in Deceit
Vampire in Defiance

Vampire in Conflict

Vampire in Chaos

Vampire in Crisis

Vampire in Control

Vampire in Charge

Family Blood Ties Set 1–3

Family Blood Ties Set 1–5

Family Blood Ties Set 4–6

Family Blood Ties Set 7–9

Sian's Solution, A Family Blood Ties Series Prequel
Novelette

Design series

Dangerous Designs

Deadly Designs

Darkest Designs

Design Series Trilogy

Standalone

In Cassie's Corner

Gem Stone (a Gemma Stone Mystery)

Time Thieves

Published Non-Fiction Books:

Career Essentials

Career Essentials: The Résumé

Career Essentials: The Cover Letter

Career Essentials: The Interview

Career Essentials: 3 in 1